Hawk and Stretch

**Other books by
Bernice Thurman Hunter:**

That Scatterbrain Booky
With Love From Booky
As Ever, Booky

A Place For Margaret
Margaret in the Middle
Margaret on her Way

The Lamplighter
The Railroader
The Firefighter

BERNICE THURMAN HUNTER

Hawk and Stretch

Cover photo by
IAN CRYSLER

Scholastic Canada Ltd.

For Bobby

*The author would like to thank Syd Charendoff,
Leading Seaman Gordon Thurman and the late
Flying Officer Roy Brand for their invaluable
assistance in the preparation of this book.*

Canadian Cataloguing in Publication Data

Hunter, Bernice Thurman
    Hawk and Stretch

ISBN 0-590-74814-9

I. Title.

PS8565.U577H39 1993   jC813'.54   C93-094008-3
PZ7.H87Ha 1993

6 5 4 3 2 1   Printed in Canada   3 4 5 6 7/9

Contents

1. September 1943 1
2. Billy's Family 8
3. Danny's Family 14
4. Letter From Arthur 27
5. "The Secret" 35
6. The Mothers 46
7. Christmas 1943 52
8. Drop Dead 69
9. The Meat Market 78
10. Return of the Hawk 85
11. The Lancaster 91
12. Good Riddance 103
13. Playing Hooky 110
14. Sick of the Bell 121
15. Capitulation 135
16. Terrible War News 146
17. Summer Holidays 158
18. Muskoka 168
19. Ghost Stories 175
20. Kinfolk 182
21. Getting Even 188

Chapter 1

September 1943

Billy Thomson leapt down the front steps and dashed across Veeny Street to call for his best friend, Sammy Watson.

Sammy flung open the door of his house and Billy heard Mrs. Watson holler from the kitchen, "Don't forget your hanky, Sammy!"

"Okay, Ma!" Sammy hollered back. Then he gave his nose a snort and wiped it on his sleeve.

"Cut that out, Sam!" Billy glared down at his friend who was about a head shorter than he was. "You wanna make me sick?"

Sammy just laughed.

Kicking a stone along the sidewalk, Billy grumbled, "I hate it when there's no 'Ex.' There's nothing to look forward to at the end of summer holidays."

"Yeah, it's rotten," agreed Sammy with another snort.

Ever since May 20, 1942, the Canadian National Exhibition grounds in Toronto had been commandeered by the armed forces, and that meant no more exhibition for the duration of the war.

The school was only a stone's throw away and the bell was ringing so they raced each other to the schoolyard and joined the lineup at the boys' door.

Moments later they were marching into their classroom to the beat of "When Johnny Canuck Comes Marching Home, Hurrah! Hurrah!" pounded out by Miss Minnie Beasley on the out-of-tune piano.

Billy and Sammy slipped quietly into two empty seats in the back row. Instantly the teacher whirled around, chalk in hand, and ordered them up to the front. Then he turned back to the blackboard and the chalk screeched as he wrote in capital letters:

TUESDAY, SEPTEMBER 8, 1943.

GRADE SEVEN.

TEACHER: OLIVER WILLIAM LITTLE, ESQUIRE.

When the class finally settled down Mr. Little dusted the chalk off his hands and began to call out the students' names from a list on his desk. Just as he was finishing roll call the door at the back of the room banged against the wall and a stranger slid into one of the empty seats.

"YOU!" Pointing with his finger, Mr. Little indicated that the newcomer should come up to the front and occupy the seat next to Billy Thomson. The boy swaggered up the aisle and plunked himself down. Billy darted him a furtive, sidelong glance and shoved over to the edge of his seat.

The teacher glared at the new boy over his horn-rimmed glasses. Those owlish spectacles, topped off by tufted grey eyebrows and combined with his initials, had long since earned him the nickname of 'The Owl.'

"Who sent you in here?" demanded The Owl.

"The principal," the boy answered, bold as brass.

"What's your name?"

"Danny."

"Do you mean Daniel?"

"Yeah."

"Daniel what?"

"Daniel Thunder."

"What in thunder kind of a name is that?" snapped Mr. Little derisively.

"Mohawk," Danny shot back defiantly. "It's really Thundercloud but my old man shortened it."

"By 'old man,' do you mean your father?"

"Yeah."

Frowning his disapproval, The Owl said, "If you mean your father, say your father. There'll be no disrespect tolerated in this class, boy. From now on watch your mouth."

Danny gave a little smirk, but said no more. Billy eyed him curiously.

He looked different from all the other boys. He had poker-straight black hair that hung down over his ears, eyes as shiny and dark as a sparrow's, and smooth brown skin that stretched over high, prominent cheekbones.

All through class the new boy exhibited a brashness and impudence that fascinated Billy. He found himself constantly watching him out of the corner of his eye. Then the bell rang for recess and the prospect of fifteen minutes of freedom drove all other thoughts out of his mind. Billy and Sammy dashed outside to play kick-the-can in a corner of the schoolyard.

They had no sooner set up the can than Sammy muttered out of the corner of his mouth, "Look who's coming!"

Billy looked and saw the new boy strutting toward them. All at once he raced in and kicked the can so hard it went flying over the chain-link fence into the girls' side of the schoolyard.

Billy felt a shiver of fear. He was a lot taller than the newcomer, but he was also as skinny as a beanpole, and his older brother, Jakey, always said that a stiff wind would blow him over.

By contrast, Danny was short and stocky, with broad shoulders and bulging biceps.

"Who's the toughest guy in this here school?" demanded Danny Thunder.

"Rock Hammer," Billy replied instantly, glad to switch Danny's attention to somebody else. "He beats me up just about every day. That's him over there." He pointed to a big, mean-looking boy who was at that very moment tormenting a little boy half his size. He had the smaller boy's arm twisted halfway up his back and was yelling at him, "Say uncle, you little twerp!"

Just then Rock happened to glance up and caught Billy pointing him out. Dropping his victim like a cat drops a mouse, he strode toward them.

Quick as a wink, Billy licked his finger and held it up in the air as if testing which way the wind was blowing, but he was too late.

As soon as Rock arrived, he balled his fist and swung at Billy. Quicker than lightning, Danny Thunder jumped between them and blocked the blow with his forearm.

"Why don't you pick on somebody your own size, you big ape?" he growled.

Rock Hammer gazed over Danny's head and stared all around. "Sure, bring him on. Where is he?"

Without warning, Danny landed a hard right to the bully's mid-section.

With a loud grunt, Rock doubled over, hugging his stomach.

"What the . . . I'll kill you, you little rat!" he yelled, and began swinging wildly.

But all he hit was empty air. Danny ducked

and danced like a boxer in the ring.

"C'mon, hit me!" he goaded him. "I dare ya to hit me. I double-dog dare ya!"

Instantly the two combatants were surrounded by a yelling circle of boys, while the girls lined up and cheered from their side of the chain-link fence.

With a vicious uppercut, Danny sent Rock sprawling. Then he jumped on the bigger boy and pinned him spread-eagled on the ground, begging for mercy.

"I give up!" blubbered Rock through split lips.

"Say uncle," yelled Danny.

"Uncle!"

"Say it again!"

"Uncle! Uncle!"

Danny let go of Rock and got up slowly. He brushed the gravel off his pants into his opponent's tear-streaked face. Then he stepped nonchalantly aside and sauntered back to where Billy and Sammy were standing with mouths gaping open.

"Now who's the toughest guy in the school?" he demanded.

"You are!" they cried in unison.

"Okay. So don't forget it," Danny said.

* * *

After school, Billy and Sammy walked up Veeny Street with their new friend.

"Are you really a Mohawk, Danny?" Billy asked hesitantly.

"One quarter, on my old man's side," Danny said, squaring his shoulders proudly.

"Then how be I call you Hawk?"

"That's okay by me. You got a nickname?"

"No. Just call me Bill."

"His whole family calls him Bingo," Sammy volunteered with a grin.

Billy groaned in embarrassment. "Only my mother calls me that, stupid!" What would a Mohawk think of a name like Bingo!

Danny looked up at Billy. "I think I'll call you Stretch," he said. "How old are you, Stretch?"

"I'm eleven," Billy said.

"Yeah? How come you're in grade seven if you're only eleven?"

" 'Cause I skipped," Billy mumbled.

"Twice! He skipped twice," Sammy said proudly, eager to be a part of the conversation.

"Yeah? Well, I'm twelve and I ain't so smart," Danny said. "But with your brains and my brawn, Stretch, I bet we'd make a great team."

"You said it, Hawk!"

Solemnly they shook hands to cement their partnership.

Feeling left out, Sammy gave a disdainful snort and went home.

Chapter 2

Billy's Family

"What's for supper, Mum?" Billy called as he let the screen door slam behind him.

"For mercy sakes, child, don't *do* that. I've got a cake in the oven," cried Fran Thomson. "There's pork sausages for supper. Now go wash yourself. You smell all hot and sweaty."

"I'm thirsty."

"Have a drink of water. Let the tap run so it'll get nice and cold."

"Can I put a chunk of ice in it, Mum?"

"Yas, but be quick about it. The longer you hold the lid open, the faster the ice melts."

The icebox was a wooden model that loaded from the top. Billy unhooked the ice pick from the nail on the side and cracked off a corner of the fifty-pound crystal block just as his brother came in the kitchen door.

Jakey handed his mother a newspaper left over from his paper route and helped himself to a spear of ice.

Fran Thomson spread the *Evening Telegram* out on the kitchen table, anxiously scanning the front page. Billy looked over her shoulder, sucking noisily on his ice chunk.

The headlines were printed in bold black letters:

CARNAGE CONTINUES AS CANADIAN TROOPS POUR INTO FRANCE!

"Thank the Lord Arthur's not in the army," murmured Fran.

"When's Arthur coming home, Mum?" asked Billy.

"When the lights come on all over the world, I guess, Bingo."

Arthur was Billy's oldest brother and he was serving in the Royal Canadian Navy. There had not been a letter from him in weeks and Billy knew his mother was worried sick about him.

"I hope the war lasts long enough for me to join up," declared Jakey, his brown eyes sparkling. "I'm going to be a gunner in a bomber."

Squinting his eye, he cocked his head and looked down the sights of an imaginary machine gun. "Rat-a-tat-a-tat-a-tat . . . Pow! Gotcha, you nutsy Nazi!" he laughed.

"I want to join up too," Billy said. "Only I want to be a pilot in the RCAF."

"You can't be nothing because you're too young and skinny," laughed Jakey, giving him a poke.

"Ow! You rat!" Billy poked him back.

"Stop it, the both of you!" cried their mother, her dark eyes bright with fear. "One of my boys away to war is all my heart can take."

She pressed her hand against her chest and then folded the paper. Fetching the iron skillet from a hook in the cellarway, Fran placed it on the Acme coal-and-gas range, in front of the pots boiling on the back burners.

Billy sniffed over his mother's shoulder as she began frying sausages.

"I could eat a horse!" he declared.

"That's because you're growing like a weed," his mother replied. "All my children are taller than me now, even my Baby-Bo-Bingo."

"Aw, Mum, cut that out!"

"Well, for land's sake, where's your funny bone? Did you leave it back at school? And by the way, how did your first day go?"

When the sausages began to sizzle, Fran gave the skillet a practised shake and they all turned over like a row of bathers browning in the sun.

"And how do you like Mr. Little?"

"He's okay, I guess. And I made a swell new friend. His name is Danny Thunder. He's one-quarter Mohawk Indian and he's tougher than Rock Hammer." He decided not to tell her about the fight. "We even gave each other nicknames. He's Hawk and I'm Stretch."

"That's nice," his mother answered absently.

Just then Billy's older sister, Bea, came in the door. She looked haggard from a long day's work at Eaton's.

"Bea-Bea . . . "

"What do you want, Billy? I always know you want something when you call me 'Bea-Bea.' "

Bea took off her pillbox hat, kicked off her spectator pumps, kissed her mum's flushed cheek, and slumped on the chair beside the stove.

"Will you learn me how to ride dad's bike after supper? I'm the only kid in Swansea who can't ride a two-wheel."

" 'Teach,' Billy, not 'learn.' You know better than that. Anyway, I don't think Dad will lend you his bike. And besides, I'm too tired. I've been on my feet all day."

"Awww!"

"Oh, I'll see. Maybe I'll feel better after supper."

"Oh, pshaw, Booky" — occasionally Fran still called her youngest daughter by her childhood nickname — "you mustn't let Billy hornswaggle you into something you're not fit for. He wraps you around his little finger. By the way," the concern in Fran's eyes changed to a twinkle, "there's something on the hall table that might lift your spirits."

"I'll get it for you, Bea," offered Billy. "You just sit there and rest up for after supper."

Sprinting through the narrow dining room of their stuck-together house, Billy returned with a letter that made his sister's eyes light up. The envelope was stamped, "Censored and Re-Sealed." Eagerly, Bea sliced it open with a table knife.

"Is it from Lorne? Read it out loud," begged Billy.

But Bea just dreamily walked away and went upstairs reading her young husband's letter from overseas. Billy felt a twinge of jealousy. It seemed that ever since she had married handsome Lorne Huntley, Bea hardly gave him the time of day.

His mother was setting the table when the rattle of his dad's bike could be heard coming up the backyard walk, then the scrape of handlebars on stucco as he leaned the ancient CCM against the house.

Billy flung open the door. Jim Thomson came in and Billy could see right away that he was tired and cranky. Deep hollows outlined his cheekbones and his fair hair was stuck to his damp forehead from the long ride home.

Billy decided to come right out with it: "Can I borrow your bike tonight, Dad?"

"No. You know I don't lend my bike to nobody, Billy. I depend on it to get me to work and back."

Billy could tell by the tone of his father's voice that there was no use begging. It would only put him in a worse mood.

I'll ask again on the weekend, he thought.

Bea came downstairs with a smile on her face and the family sat down around the table.

Billy wolfed down crispy sausages, green peas, orange carrot rings and fluffy mashed potatoes glistening with golden brown gravy. Then he got up to go over to Sammy's.

"Wait a minute, young man. You haven't asked to be excused," his mother reminded him. "And you haven't had your pudding yet."

"Stoopid!" snapped Jakey, helping himself to cake and custard. Then, after swallowing the first creamy spoonful, he added, "Mmmmm, good supper, Mum."

Billy noticed that Jakey always complimented his mother's cooking, and no matter how weary she was, it always brought a smile to her face.

Sometimes he worried that Jakey might be his mother's favourite. After all, Jakey was the only one of the five children who took after her side of the family. He had the Coles' brown eyes and dark curly hair, and Billy knew this pleased his mother, because she often mentioned it.

As he headed over to the Watsons' house after eating his pudding and asking to be excused, he found himself wishing that Danny Thunder lived across the street instead of Sammy Watson.

Chapter 3

Danny's Family

Billy didn't have to worry about Rock Hammer anymore. Even if Danny was nowhere in sight, Rock knew it was as much as his life was worth to pick on Billy again.

Billy couldn't quite figure out why Danny had chosen him as a best friend, since they were as different as day and night. Still, he was proud as punch about it.

One day he took Danny home to meet his mother. As they came into the yard through the back gate, they heard the screech of the pulley-line. Fran Thomson was standing on the wooden stoop taking in the washing. At her feet the wicker basket overflowed with sun-bleached clothes.

"Don't just stand there like a clod," she said irritably. "Carry the basket in for me." She was always like that on washdays. Tired and cranky.

Billy hoisted the basket up, looking a bit embarrassed, "Mum . . . this here is my friend, Danny Thunder. Remember I told you about him? Can he stay for supper?"

Fran Thomson stepped hurriedly down from the stoop. "For mercy sakes, Billy, you know we only have potluck on washdays."

Billy looked even more embarrassed and Danny started backing away. Then Fran, not wanting to hurt the boy's feelings, said, "I'm sorry, Danny. I haven't got enough to go around tonight. But you'll be more than welcome another time."

"He don't eat much, do you, Hawk?" persisted Billy.

"Yeah I do. I eat tons," Danny said.

"Well, I haven't got tons." Fran Thomson laughed in spite of herself. "Maybe later in the week."

"How about you come to my house then, Stretch?"

"Can I, Mum?"

"Well, I don't know. Where do you live?"

Now Fran Thomson inspected Billy's new friend more closely.

"In the flat above the Cut-Rate," answered Danny.

"The Cut-Rate Meat Market?"

"Yeah. We just moved there. My ma's the new cashier."

"Your mother works?"

Billy caught a trace of envy in his mother's question.

"Yeah."

"What does your father do?"

"Ahhh . . . " Danny looked down and shuffled his feet. "He's in business for hisself," he muttered.

"My land!" Fran was instantly impressed. "That does sound important. Well, phone your mother. If she says it's all right by her, then I guess it's all right by me."

Billy dropped the wash basket on the kitchen linoleum and pulled Danny by the shirt-sleeve into the narrow dining room where a black wooden telephone box was mounted on the wall.

Danny dialled, muttered a few words, then hung up.

"Ma says sure," he announced.

So off they ran up Veeny Street.

As they passed a house on the corner of Veeny and Mayberry Streets, they noticed some words had been splashed with white paint on the tall board fence.

"NAZI GO HOME!" blared the ugly message.

"Holy geez!" cried Danny. "Does a kraut live there?"

"No! That's Mr. Vierkoetter's house."

"Vierkoetter. Ain't that a German name?"

"Yeah. But Mr. Vierkoetter's a Canadian. And he's a hero. Don't you know about him, Hawk?"

"Never heard of him."

"Well, he won the first Wrigley marathon swim at the Exhibition in 1927. He was nicknamed the Black Shark."

"How come you know all that stuff, Stretch? You weren't even born then."

"No, but my mum told me. Besides, Mr. Vierkoetter is my swim coach. And he says I'm the best in his class. You wanna take swimming lessons with me, Hawk?"

"No. I hate water. C'mon, let's get going."

The two boys ran the rest of the way to Bloor Street.

As they entered the meat market, the bell over the door jangled. Skirting the lineup of customers at the wicket, Danny led the way across the sawdust covered floor to a door at the back.

Billy followed Danny up a long dark staircase into a big bright room.

The first thing to catch Billy's eye was a coloured painting of an Indian chief in full headdress hanging by a wire on the wall.

"Who's that?" he asked.

"That's Chief Thundercloud. He's my great-great-grandpa, or something like that," Danny shrugged.

Now Billy scanned the rest of the room. There was a big picnic-style table in the middle, and against one wall was a Kitchen Queen gas range and a Servel refrigerator with the motor on top. A stack of boxes leaned in one corner, and in another there stood a tall brass stand with a huge birdcage suspended from it. Inside the cage was a puffy green parrot. He cocked his head and stared at them with one beady yellow eye.

"SCRAM!" screeched the parrot.

"Shut up, Angel!" hissed Danny. "You'll wake up the old man."

A man lay dozing on a couch in front of a plate glass window that looked out onto Bloor Street. His arms were folded across his chest and he was snoring like a chain saw. He had long black hair like Danny.

"Who's that guy?" whispered Billy.

"My old man . . . my dad," explained Danny.

"Where's your mum?"

"Didn't you see her? She was in the cashier's booth. She'll come up later and rustle up some grub."

"What'll we do till she comes?" Billy continued to whisper.

"We could play poker."

"I don't know how."

Danny chuckled at that and his black eyes glittered.

"You got any money on you, Stretch?"

Billy dug into the pocket of his breeches and came up with a quarter.

"Is this enough?"

"It'll do for a start."

Danny fetched a well-worn deck of cards from a

shelf above the stove and the boys sat opposite each other at the picnic table.

"Now pay attention, Stretch."

Danny shuffled the deck expertly and then explained the game as he dealt the cards.

Billy listened carefully and easily won the first hand.

Danny darted him a suspicious look.

"You sure you never played poker before?" he demanded.

"Sure, I'm sure," Billy responded.

"Beginner's luck, then," grunted Danny.

"Can we have another game before supper?" Billy asked, rubbing his hands together gleefully.

"Okay," Danny agreed, slapping the deck of cards down in front of Billy. "Now shut up and deal!"

Billy shuffled awkwardly, flipping and dropping cards all over the place. Then he dealt them helter-skelter over the table.

"This time will be different," Danny promised.

Three hands later, Billy had won every cent Danny had.

"Geez!" Danny groaned. "I forgot you're the brains of this outfit." He swept up the cards and returned them to the shelf. "After supper I'll sic you onto my brothers. We'll beat the pants offa them and split the spoils. Okay, Stretch?"

"Sure, Hawk. Anything you say. And you can have your money back." Billy pushed him the little pile of change. "I was only playing for fun, not for keeps."

Danny pushed it roughly back again.

"I always play for keeps," he growled.

Suddenly the door flew open and Danny's mother came blowing into the kitchen like a thunderstorm.

She seemed to Billy to be about twice the size of his own mother, with round dimpled cheeks, bright red lips that overlapped her mouth and a head full of tangled blond curls.

"Where's your brothers? Can't you even open a tin can? Wake up your good-for-nothing father. Do I have to do everything around here?"

"Yak! Yak! Yak!" screeched the parrot.

"Shut up, Angel!" yelled Mrs. Thunder, giving the cage a shake.

Clinging to his spar, Angel bobbed up and down and squawked swear words that would have made a sailor blush.

"I'll fix you, you varmint," Mrs. Thunder cried triumphantly as she threw a black felt cloth over the bouncing cage. Like magic, the saucy bird shut up.

Billy laughed, and that's when Mrs. Thunder noticed him, tall and skinny, leaning awkwardly against the table, his right foot tucked behind his left ankle.

"Who in the world are you?" she bawled.

"This here's Stretch Thomson, Ma. I told you he was coming for supper."

Now it was Danny's turn to feel embarrassed.

"Oh, sure. Don't mind me, kiddo."

She gave Billy a welcoming smile as she got four large tins of spaghetti down from the shelf above the stove and plunked them on the table.

"Where do you live, Stretch Thomson?" she asked pleasantly as she searched the table drawer for a can opener.

"On Veeny Street, near the school," Billy replied.

"Thomson. Thomson. Don't know anyone by that name."

Mrs. Thunder cranked open the four tins and dumped the contents into a big iron kettle on the stove. Then she threw in a large bowlful of raw hamburger that she had brought up from the meat market and stirred it vigorously into the spaghetti with a giant wooden spoon. When she was finished mixing the concoction, she covered the pot with an inverted plate and turned the gas on full blast.

"Thomson," she repeated. "I used to live in Swansea when I was a girl, but I don't remember any Thomsons."

"My mum's unmarried name was Cole," explained Billy. "My great-grandpa Cole was one of the first settlers in Swansea."

"Now that rings a bell. By any chance would you be related to Mr. Bill Cole?"

"Yeah. He used to be my grandpa when he was alive. He lived on Windermere Avenue in the cement-block house."

"Oh. I didn't know he'd gone home."

Billy understood what she meant, because his mother used the same expression about where dead people go.

"He was a lovely man," continued Mrs. Thunder. "God rest his soul."

Just then, the back door to the kitchen banged open and a boy with dark hair like Danny's clattered in. He marched right over to the cage and whipped the cover off.

"Ihay Angelay!" he yelled.

"Ihay! Ihay! Ihay!" squawked the excited bird.

Billy looked completely baffled.

"What the heck did he say?" he asked Danny.

"Aw, that's my brother Austin. Aussie, we call him. He's nuts. He thinks he's smart 'cause he can talk pig latin."

A few minutes later in came two more boys. Danny introduced them as his brothers Ralphie and Bevan. Billy noticed that the two oldest were dark like Danny and their father but Bevan, the youngest, was fair-haired and blue-eyed like their mother.

"This here's Stretch Thomson," Danny said.

Ralph and Aussie just stared and grunted, but Bevan gave Billy a wide smile that showed his mother's dimples.

When the spaghetti began spewing red-hot juice from underneath the dancing plate, Mrs. Thunder dumped it, with a few colourful expletives, into a huge mixing bowl. She placed the bowl on the table and beside it plunked a loaf of bread and a pound of soft butter leaning sideways on a saucer.

"Soup's on!" she bellowed, giving her snoozing husband a cuff on the ear. There was a mad scramble as the boys jockeyed for seats on the benches.

Ignoring the confusion, the parents drew up chairs at either end of the table, and they all dug in.

The food disappeared in two minutes flat. If Danny hadn't filled both their bowls and grabbed two chunks of bread, Billy was sure he wouldn't have gotten a bite to eat.

Mr. Thunder didn't say a word during the entire meal. Finally, after carefully wiping his bowl clean with a heel of bread, he belched and grinned and asked his wife, "What's for dessert, Snookey?"

Snookey! Billy could not believe his ears. In all his life he had never heard his father call his mother a pet name.

"Dessert! Dessert!" repeated Mrs. Thunder.

"Dessert! Dessert!" mocked the parrot.

Jumping up, Mrs. Thunder began clattering the dishes into the porcelain sink that clung to the wall beside the stove.

"I've been working my fingers to the bone in that blasted meat market from morning till night," she ranted, "and you've got the gall to ask for dessert? What have you been doing with yourself all day long, you lazy lump?"

Billy held his breath expecting a big fight to break out. But instead Mr. Thunder just bellowed with laughter and slapped his knee.

"Keep your shirt on, woman," he said. "I'll take care of it."

Then he leaned back on the hind legs of his chair, reached inside his pants pocket, and pulled out a crumpled two-dollar bill.

"Here, Danny-boy, you and Skinny there slide down to the ice-cream parlour and get a quart of vanilla."

"Oh, fart! Ice-cream again," exclaimed his wife. Then, catching Billy's startled blink, she laughed and added, "Excuse my French, kiddo!"

Mrs. Thunder handed Danny a green glass bowl and said, "Now you make sure that old skinflint fills that bowl to overflowing, 'cause we got company. And hurry back before it melts."

Billy had never eaten such a huge dish of ice cream before. Rubbing his bulging stomach, he declared, "That was a swell dessert, Mr. Thunder. And the spaghetti was good, too, Mrs. Thunder."

Dimpling at the compliment, Violet Thunder gave Billy's lean cheek a pinch.

"Glad you liked it, kiddo. It's my I-talian special-ty. Tell your ma I said you're welcome anytime."

After the table was cleared and wiped off, Danny artfully suggested a game of poker. His brothers eagerly agreed and scrambled back into their seats.

Giving Billy the high sign with a raised eyebrow, Danny dealt the cards.

In short order Billy won three quarters, two dimes and a nickel.

"Where did you learn to play poker?" said Ralphie suspiciously.

"I showed him," grinned Danny, snapping the cards between his thumbs. "He only learned today."

"Bull!" sneered Ralphie.

"No, honest!" Billy's voice went up an octave and his heart skipped a beat. "I never played poker in my life before. We always play euchre at our house."

"Bull!" chorused the three brothers.

"Bull! Bull!" squawked Angel.

Suddenly Danny scraped back his chair, slapped the cards on the table and threw the cover over the birdcage.

"C'mon, Stretch," he said. "Let's get outta here."

Billy's heart was still flip-flopping as they hurried down the back stairs.

In the laneway Danny stopped and held out his hand.

"Okay, kid. Gimme my cut," he demanded.

"Sure, Hawk!" Billy happily shared his winnings. "Are your brothers really mad at me?" he asked anxiously.

"Yeah. But you got nothing to worry about as long as I'm around."

Billy was only partly reassured. What might

they do to him when Danny wasn't around?

* * *

Later, on his way home, Billy saw that the ugly words were still scrawled across Mr. Vierkoetter's fence. So he ran the rest of the way, got some whitewash from the cellar, and went back and painted them out.

Chapter 4

Letter From Arthur

"Mum, there's a letter!" Billy scooped the V-Mail envelope up off the floor where it had landed when the mailman pushed it through the slot in the front door.

Mrs. Thomson dropped her dustpan and dirt went flying.

"Oh, the Lord be praised!" she cried as she took the long-awaited letter.

She turned it over and traced Arthur's spidery handwriting lovingly. Billy noticed that her hands were trembling.

"Read it out loud," suggested Dad. It was Saturday afternoon, so he was home from work.

Mrs. Thomson read the back of the envelope in a quavering voice, "From Leading Seaman Arthur

Thomson, V 27240, H.M.C.S. (Censored)."

"What's been blacked out, and what does the V stand for, Mum?" asked Billy.

Jim Thomson answered his question. "The name of his ship is censored for security. And the V stands for volunteer. Our Arthur didn't wait to be conscripted. Nor did I in the big war."

Fran Thomson began ripping at the envelope.

"Oh, mercy, my fingers are all thumbs," she said.

She finally got the envelope open without tearing the letter inside and began to read:

> *Somewhere in England.*
> *October 12, 1943.*
>
> *Dear Mum and Dad and Family,*
>
> *I'm sorry I haven't written in such a long time, but I've been laid up in the hospital here in (censored).*

Billy's mother gasped and her hand flew to her throat.

> *Don't worry, Mum, I'm not wounded. I've just had pneumonia. And I'm on the mend now, so don't get upset.*
>
> *This is what happened. A German U-boat torpedoed our destroyer and badly damaged it in the bow. Lucky it wasn't the stern, or we'd have sunk for sure. I was off duty at the time and before I knew it the captain was ordering everybody overboard.*

It was a calm day and the Atlantic was as smooth as the Grenadier Pond. That sounds nice, but actually these days it's one of the most hazardous times to be at sea. We always feel safer when the ship is rolling in rough waters. It's much harder for a U-boat to attack then.

Anyway, we got our life jackets on and went over the side. The carley floats (they're something like rafts) had already been lowered, so we clung to them and waited to be rescued. We were in the water for over two hours and that's how I got pneumonia.

But like I said I'm okay now. I've been moved from the hospital to (censored) to convalesce, and, boy, are the nurses ever pretty here. English girls all have pink and white complexions and beautiful blue eyes like the King's wife.

"Humph!" Mrs. Thomson muttered with a jealous flash of her dark brown eyes. "I hope Arthur doesn't get taken in by those limey girls. I don't want him coming home with a war bride. He's much too young."

"Oh, Mum. He's older than me. Keep reading," Bea said.

Last night there was a bad air raid on a big city. I can't tell you which city, but the raid was a dilly. I think Dad will get the message.

"That's London he's talking about," Mr. Thomson

said, a spark of excitement in his voice. "Dilly would be short for Piccadilly. I can picture it as plain as if it was yesterday. Piccadilly Circus."

"Oh, hush," his wife snapped. "World War One is history now. And it wasn't the war to end all wars like you always said it would be. Now let's hear what more our Arthur's got to say."

Jim Thomson clamped his mouth shut in a tight line. He hated to be reminded that he had been wrong about that prediction.

Mrs. Thomson continued to read, her voice steadier now that she knew her son was safe.

Tonight there's going to be a dance in the barracks and the medics say I'm well enough to go. I can hardly wait to get back into my navy blues. Trouble is, I have to get them taken in. I haven't been in uniform for over a month, so this morning I tried on my bell-bottoms to see how they fit. The waist is much too big because I've lost over a stone (that's English weight for fourteen pounds).

"Well, stones or pounds, it's too much weight for a slim boy like my Arthur to lose. He must be skin and bones," worried Fran.

"Read more, Mum," begged Jakey. "You keep interrupting the story."

"Is it just a story?" Billy frowned his disappointment. "I thought it was all real."

"Geez!" Jakey slapped himself on the forehead.

"How come you say such dumb things when you're supposed to be so smart?"

"It's real all right, Billy," Bea assured him. "Lorne's last letter scared the wits out of me. He was lucky to get back from his last mission alive. I only wish he was safe in a convalescent camp instead of flying across the channel every night of the week."

"But, Bea," put in Jakey with a mischievous grin, "then he might meet one of them beautiful English nurses Arthur's so crazy about, and never come back."

Bursting into tears, Bea walloped Jakey and ran upstairs.

"Shame on you, Jakey," Mrs. Thomson scolded, ignoring the red marks spreading across his cheek. "Lorne would never do such a dastardly thing."

"Aw, Mum, read the rest," begged Billy.

He really missed his big brother. He and Jakey were too close in age to get along. Their mother said it was as bad as raising a cat and dog together.

The food here isn't so good because the limeys always overcook everything. I really miss your swell dinners, Mum, (Fran nodded her head in satisfaction) especially now that I have to eat as much as possible to try and regain the weight I lost. I'm really anxious to get back into action, but I won't be called back to active duty until I pass my medical and (censored).

"For mercy sakes, half the page is blacked out. It's

hard to make head or tail of what Arthur's trying to say."

"Well, try anyway," grunted Mr. Thomson impatiently.

Fran Thomson gave a derisive little sniff and continued.

By the way, did I mention that the king and queen visited the hospital while I was there? And the king stopped by my bed and wished me a speedy recovery. I managed to say, 'Thank you, Your Majesty,' but I was too weak to salute.

"Gosh, imagine, our Arthur actually talking to the King of England," marvelled Billy.

Well, that's my big news. Tell Jakey and Billy I'll bring them souvenirs if this war ever gets over. But it doesn't look too promising, because the Jerrys (censored).

"Oh, pshaw," Mrs. Thomson complained, "more blackouts."

Then she finished the letter.

With love to all,
Your son and brother, Arthur.
P.S. Mum, could you send me some nuts from Aunt Susan's store? Tell her thanks and giant cashews are my favourites.
P.P.S. Be sure Willa (Willa was the oldest in the family) *reads this letter, because when I get back on board the (censored) I might not have time to write to her and Clifford. I hope they're*

both well and enjoying their new house.

A.

"How come Cliffie isn't in the war, Mum?" asked Billy.

"Because he has a weak heart and the army turned him down. He's doing his bit by working at DeHavilland, making airplanes for brave airmen like Lorne to fly."

"How many times do I have to tell you that Lorne is a navigator, not a pilot, Mum?" said Bea peevishly.

She had come back downstairs, but she was still upset over Jakey's remark.

"They must have tons of money to afford a house," remarked Billy.

"Well, that's why Willa works at the Kodak plant. It takes two pay packets to buy a home nowadays. The price of houses has skyrocketed since the war," Fran said.

"How much did they give for that little place of theirs?" Jim asked.

"I'm not sure. Willa is close-mouthed about money."

"Well, Annie Dewsbury, one of the girls in my office, bought a house on the same street as Willa and she told me they paid $4,500 for it," put in Bea.

"Good Glory!" declared Jim Thomson. "They must have more money than brains."

Fran folded the precious letter and tucked it into her apron pocket.

"Well, I'm not fussy about the new houses they're building these days. The kitchens are too poky. But I wouldn't turn my nose up at this old place."

She looked around, redecorating with her eyes.

"I wonder what Billy and Maude would want for it."

Billy and Maude Sundy were an unmarried brother and sister who owned the house the Thomsons lived in. They charged a very modest rent because Grandpa Cole, Fran Thomson's father, had been their lifelong friend.

"Whatever it is, we can't afford it," snapped Mr. Thomson.

That remark put Fran in a bad mood for days.

Billy hated it when his parents were mad at each other, because the nagging and grumbling would often lead to a full-blown fight and the house would be filled with gloom.

So to escape from the angry dark cloud, he found himself spending more time at Danny Thunder's place above the Cut-Rate Meat Market.

Chapter 5

"The Secret"

The Owl had kept Danny in after school. Billy was waiting for him outside the boys' door when Rock Hammer jumped down the wide cement steps and landed with a thud at Billy's feet. He gave Billy a menacing glare, but that was all. He didn't dare punch him like he used to do.

The sky was darkening down and a sleety rain had begun to fall, so Billy went up the steps and stood just inside the double doors. He knew he'd be in trouble if he got caught, because loitering on school property wasn't allowed after four o'clock.

Miss Mather, the grade one teacher, came down the hall, her spike heels clickety-clicking on the wide board floor. Billy opened the heavy oak doors for her, his heart lurching. Miss Mather was a real good-looker and Billy liked to imagine that he'd marry her someday. When she saw how nasty the weather was, she stopped to tie a red silk kerchief over her wavy chestnut hair.

"Why are you still here, Billy?" she asked, favouring him with a pearly white smile.

"I'm waiting for Danny Thunder. He had to stay in."

"Well, don't wait around too long," she warned, then ran down the steps and across the schoolyard to where her 1938 green Durant was parked. Billy held his breath, expecting her to slip on the icy gravel, but she didn't so his plan to dash to her rescue was thwarted.

Danny Thunder came striding down the hall, his face as dark as a thundercloud.

"The Owl's a jerk!" he declared, his black eyes flashing.

"Yeah," agreed Billy. Then he added, "Is it okay if I come home with you again, Hawk?" He had already been there two days in a row.

"Sure."

Billy thought Danny was lucky because he never had to ask his mother first when he wanted to bring someone home for supper. Billy wouldn't dare do that.

As the two boys ran up Veeny Street, they saw Billy's Aunt Ellie out chopping ice.

"Hi, Aunt Ellie!" called Billy.

Ellie waved and smiled.

Then on Durie Street, there was his Aunt Milly sprinkling salt on the sidewalk. She was wearing spike-heeled galoshes.

"Hi, Aunt Milly!"

"Halloo yourself, Bingo!" she answered cheerily.

"How come you know everybody?" asked Danny curiously.

"Because nearly everybody in Swansea is my relation," explained Billy proudly.

As they turned into the back lane behind the butcher shop they saw a Chinese laundryman with a pigtail taking in washing off a line that zigzagged back and forth across the lane.

"Who's that?" asked Billy curiously.

"The Chinaman. He's got the shop next door," Danny explained. "He does all our washing."

"Doesn't your mum do her own washing?"

"Nah. She says she'd rather work late at the meat market and make extra money than be a washer-woman."

Billy frowned. He'd never thought of his mother as a washerwoman. Yet he'd seen her, every Monday, lugging the heavy loads of wet washing up the cellar stairs and breathlessly hanging everything on the pulley-line, no matter what the weather.

The laundryman, his mouth full of clothespins, shot them a wary glance.

Embarrassed to be caught staring, Billy looked

quickly away and his eyes lighted on a mud-spattered cellar window. Leaning over, he caught a glimpse of Mr. Thunder holding up a bottle to a bare light bulb.

"Hey! What's your dad doing down there, Hawk?"

Suddenly Danny gave Billy a shove that sent him sprawling onto the gravel laneway.

"Hey! Whatcha do that for, Hawk?"

" 'Cause if my old man catches us spying on him, he'll brain the both of us," Danny said, giving Billy a hand up.

"Why? What's he doing?"

Billy brushed the wet gravel off his school breeches. Danny pushed Billy ahead, out of sight of the window.

"If I let you in on a secret, can you keep your yap shut?"

"Sure!"

"He's making hootch," Danny said in a hoarse whisper.

"What's hootch?" Billy whispered back.

"Don't you know nothing?"

"I never heard of it."

"It's whiskey."

"Whiskey!"

"For Pete's sake shut up!"

Danny's dark eyes darted furtively up and down the lane. The laundryman had disappeared. He yanked Billy by the coat sleeve through the doorway leading up the back stairs.

In the dark stairwell he said, "Listen, Stretch. My old man's a bootlegger, see!"

"Bootlegger!"

"Geez! Keep quiet. Do you have to repeat everything I say?

For a split-second Billy pictured Mr. Thunder busy making boots in the basement. But the look of indignation on his friend's face told him he was dead wrong about that.

"You have to swear you won't tell nobody," Danny said.

"I swear," promised Billy.

"Especially your old man and old lady."

Billy winced.

"They won't tell," he said.

"They might. Your folks are what my old lady would call strait-laced."

"Yeah, but they're not mean."

"I know. But they might think it's their duty to tell because what my old man does is illegal. So if they decided to sing . . . "

"Sing?" Billy queried.

"Geez, Stretch, you're dumb as a doornail. Sing means snitch, squeal, blab to the cops. And if they did that, my old man would end up in the slammer for sure."

"Really?"

"Yeah, really."

"Well, is that his job? I remember once you told my mum that your dad was in business for hisself. Is that his business?"

"Yeah. But don't forget your promise. If you squeal, your name is mud. Got it?" Danny's voice was cold as sleet.

"Got it," agreed Billy with a shiver as he followed Danny up the stairs and into the kitchen.

"Hi there, Danny Boy!" squawked the parrot.

"Shut up, Angel!" returned Danny.

They hung their coats on the hook behind the door and Danny suggested a game of crokinole.

"Sure," agreed Billy, relieved that Danny didn't sound mad anymore.

Danny won three games in a row.

Just as they finished the third game, Mrs. Thunder came puffing up the front stairs from the meat market. Her blond hair was in disarray and her lipstick was all smudged. She pinched Billy's cheek in greeting and cracked Danny over the head with her wide gold wedding band.

"Where's your brothers? Get rid of that board and lay the table. Are you staying for supper tonight, Peaches?"

"Yes, thanks," Billy grinned. He sure did like Mrs. Thunder. And her suppers were more fun than a picnic.

This time she boiled a big pot of water and threw into it a huge package of macaroni. When it was done, she drained the water off, added two large cans of stewed tomatoes, a handful of herbs and spices and a stream of Tabasco sauce.

By the time they all sat down around the picnic table Billy was starving, so he scooped up a big spoonful and was about to put it in his mouth when Danny grabbed his hand in midair.

"Not so fast there, Stretch!" he cried. "This here's hot stuff. It's another one of Ma's specialties; we call it Ma Thunder's revenge."

Mr. Thunder bellowed with laughter. "My Snookey's macaroni will grow hair on your chest, Skinny, and that's for sure."

He had dubbed Billy Skinny from day one. Billy didn't mind, just so long as Mr. Thunder liked him. Both Danny's parents seemed to like him a lot. His brothers were another story.

Aussie always seemed to look right through him, Ralphie stuck his foot out to trip him at every opportunity and Bevan made it plain he was jealous of his mother's affection for Billy. Billy knew what it was like to be the youngest in the family, so he tried extra hard to be nice to Bevan.

After supper, Billy jumped up to help Mrs. Thunder with the dishes, which was something he'd never do for his own mother.

It was her own fault, he decided, because, as she put it herself, she was 'too pernickety' — and proud of it! If a plate came out of the dishpan with a speck of food stuck on it, she'd grab it out of the wiper's hand and plop it right back in the water.

Mrs. Thunder, on the other hand, would just laugh and say, "Clean it off on the dishtowel. What do you think I'm paying you for?"

That night the whole family gathered around the picnic table to play crokinole. The board fairly sizzled as the black wooden discs whizzed between the steel posts.

Billy lost every game and Aussie laughed and jeered, "Oybay ouyay areay aay ottenray rokinolecay layerpay."

"Ayay! Iay uresay amay!" agreed Billy.

Aussie stared at him open-mouthed. "Who taught you how to talk pig latin?" he snarled.

"You did. I learned by listening to you. I'm good at languages. You must be too, Aussie."

Aussie gave him a sceptical look, then he smiled grudgingly at the compliment.

Several hours went by and time was forgotten in the boisterous excitement of the game. Mrs. Thunder got up to put the kettle on and noticed something peculiar.

"Whose coat is that hanging on the phone?" she demanded.

"Not mine!" yelled all the boys in unison.

"Not mine!" squawked Angel.

"Liars!" she scoffed.

With a guffaw, Mr. Thunder stretched out his long

arm and removed the offending coat, revealing the black, horn-shaped receiver dangling on its cord down the wall. He got up and replaced it, and the phone rang instantly.

He picked the receiver up and bellowed, "Thunder!" into the mouthpiece.

Angel leapt with a crash to the side of his cage yelling "Thunder! Thunder!" and Mrs. Thunder shouted, "Elwood, you flaming idiot, how many times do I have to tell you not to answer the phone like that?" as she threw the cover over the rocking cage.

Mr. Thunder pressed a finger in one ear and listened with the other.

"It's for you, Skinny," he said.

Billy took the phone and said, "Hello."

"Billy Thomson!" His mother's voice crackled over the wire. "Why didn't you let me know where you were going? It's ten o'clock and I've been phoning for hours. And your father is out looking for you this very minute. You'd better get home here before he does, or he'll blister your hide with the razor strop!"

"Okay, Mum!"

Slamming the receiver down, he grabbed his coat off the door.

"I gotta go. My dad's on the warpath and my mum's all upset. Thanks for the swell supper, Mrs. Thunder."

"You're welcome, Peaches!" she called after him as he took the back stairs two at a time.

Galloping home, he tumbled through the kitchen door in five minutes flat.

"Go to bed, Billy," cried Bea, "and I'll tell Dad you're sound asleep!"

"Is he that mad?"

"Yas he's that mad." His mother came running from the front window, her hand over her heart. "And so am I, you thoughtless whelp. I thought something terrible had happened to you. Why do you go up there to that flat above the Cut-Rate instead of coming home? What's so special about that bunch? Is Danny's mother a better cook than I am?"

"No, Mum. But they have fun."

"Fun! Fun!" she cried, wringing her hands. "Don't talk to me about fun. You'll get up those stairs right now if you know what's good for you."

Billy did not need to be told twice. He sprinted up the stairs and scrambled into his pyjamas. Then he leapt into the bed in the boys' room, pulled the sheet over his head and lay perfectly still. When he heard the pounding of his father's approaching footsteps, he started to snore. He had learned how from Mr. Thunder: long rumbling snores that billowed out the bed sheet.

Suddenly the door flew open and the bulb in the ceiling burst into light. It glowed eerily through the white sheet, even penetrating Billy's tightly squeezed eyelids. For minutes that seemed like hours, the only sound Billy heard was his own snoring. Then, at last, the light clicked off and the door clacked shut. Blackness covered Billy like a velvet blanket. He sighed with relief and stopped snoring.

He knew he was lucky to have escaped a thrashing. Actually, although he and Jakey had heard many times the stories told by their older brother and sisters about the razor strop, neither of them had ever felt its sting. Their mother said that was because their father had gone soft in his old age.

Still, Billy wished his father wasn't so strict and his mother wasn't such a worry-wart. Why couldn't they be more like Danny's parents? Danny and his brothers could do anything they liked and nobody cared. Why, only last Saturday Danny had asked him if he could go to the midnight show at the Esquire. And he had begged for his mother's permission.

"For mercy sakes, no!" Fran Thomson had bristled at the request. "You're just a little boy. It's not safe to be out all hours of the night."

Danny hadn't even bothered asking his mother. He just went, and when he got home at two in the morning, he told Billy later, the whole house was dead to the world.

Chapter 6

The Mothers

"Don't you dare put your nose out that door for a week!" Jim Thomson had ordered his youngest son after the late night episode. "You come straight home from school and you stay home."

Reluctantly Billy said goodbye to Danny in the laneway and went in the back door.

Nobody was home, so he dragged out his history book and opened it on the dining room table. Billy hardly ever needed to do homework. But he really disliked English history, with all its kings and queens and wars and dates, so today he hadn't bothered listening when The Owl had droned on about the War of the Roses. Now he had to catch up. Still, that was not a problem. Catching up was easy for Billy because he had such an exceptional memory.

All he had to do was read something a couple of times and he'd remember it. It was Bea who had discovered this phenomenon when he was six years old. His father had read him the story of Uncle Wiggley from the *Evening Telegram*, and the next day he had repeated it to Bea, word for word.

Jakey came in from high school, hung his windbreaker in the cellarway, and asked, "Where's Mum?"

"Dunno," Billy shrugged.

"Did she go downtown?"

"How should I know?"

"How'd you like a fat lip?" Jakey got a kick out of being the bossy big brother now that Arthur was away. "There's no note on the curtain," he observed.

"Then she didn't go downtown," Billy said.

It was Fran Thomson's habit to leave a note of instructions pinned to the kitchen curtain when she went downtown. Usually she went on Eaton's Opportunity Day, because that was when she found the best bargains.

Jakey had just finished making himself a white-sugar sandwich when the front door opened and his mother blew in on a gust of wind.

"Hello the house!" she called out as she removed her snowy galoshes and set them on a pad of newspapers on the hall floor. Then she hung her brown wool coat on the wall rack. "Brrr, that east wind bodes no good," she shivered as she hurried through the dining room and into the kitchen.

"What's for supper, Mum?" Jakey asked, brushing the grains of sugar off his mouth. "I'm starved."

"Is that all you've got to say . . . what's for supper?"

"Where'd you go, Mum?" asked Billy, thumping his history book shut.

"That's for me to know and you to find out," she joked.

"Aww, c'mon, Mum."

"Oh, all right, Bingo," she laughed as she ducked her head through the hole in her apron and tied the strings at the back. Then she untied a parcel of meat and put it in the mixing bowl. "I went to visit Violet Thunder."

"Who the heck is she?" asked Jakey as he pinched some raw hamburger out of the bowl.

"Merciful heavens, don't do that!" cried his mother, giving his fingers a crack with the blunt edge of a knife. "How many times do I have to tell you that raw meat is full of maggots."

Billy gagged, then snitched a carrot and snapped it between his teeth. "Is that Danny's mother's name . . . Violet?"

"Yas. Now isn't that a pretty name? Mumma and Puppa's favourite flowers were violets. They used to go off to the woods together to gather them in springtime. I can still picture the eggcups full of blue violets on our window sill."

Little things often reminded Fran Thomson of her long-dead parents, but her children were tired of the old stories.

"Why did you go to see Hawk's mother, Mum?"

"Well, because . . . " Fran chopped up an onion and added it along with some bread crumbs to the meat in the mixing bowl. "I wanted to see for myself what kind of people that boy Danny comes from. So I bought my meat at the Cut-Rate for a change, and when I paid for it at the wicket, I introduced myself. Then Violet invited me to the tea shop next door to the Chinese laundry and we had a nice chat."

Billy glanced at her with misgivings. He tried to picture Mrs. Thunder through his mother's eyes, with her bleached yellow hair and her bright red lips wider than her mouth.

"What did you think, Mum?" he asked anxiously. He hoped Mrs. Thunder hadn't said "bloody" or any of the other rude words he knew his mother would not like.

Fran cracked an egg on the side of the bowl and began stirring it into the meat mixture.

"I found Violet Thunder to be a good, hardworking soul," she said, adding salt and pepper and sage. "And she told me she rules her tribe of boys like a sergeant-major. Now, that's a woman after my own heart. I could take some lessons from her. And she's mighty fond of you, Billy. She called you Peaches and said you're the nicest boy Danny ever brought home."

"I'm glad you like her, Mum." Billy heaved a sigh of relief. "Mr. Thunder calls her Snookey."

Fran Thomson yelped with laughter as she popped the meatloaf into the oven and began scrubbing potatoes at the sink.

"And another good thing came of our chat," she continued breathlessly, her cheeks flushed from hurrying. "Violet and I have agreed to exchange ration coupons. She's going to trade me her meat coupons for my sugar coupons. I've got extra, since your father and I don't take sugar in our tea. Of course, I'll have to be sure to save enough for my Christmas baking. But at least I've got Arthur's parcel off. That's the main thing. Oh, I hope he gets it in time. To think this will be his first Christmas away from home."

The faraway expression in her eyes told Billy that her thoughts had suddenly gone out to sea, so he didn't ask any more questions. He was just glad that Danny's big, jolly, boisterous mother had made a good impression on his own strait-laced little mother.

But he couldn't help but wonder what his father would think of Mr. Thunder, especially if he found out what he did for a living. He knew that Danny's big, hearty, black-haired dad would make his own small-boned, fair-haired father look like a featherweight by comparison. Well, maybe if he were lucky the two would never meet.

* * *

Billy and Danny didn't see much of each other outside of school hours during December because they both found work for Christmas. Danny delivered meat for the Cut-Rate and Billy delivered papers for the *Toronto Star*.

Practically everyone in Swansea took the *Evening Telegram* from Jakey, so Billy didn't have many customers. Still, he earned a cent for each of the three-cent papers that he delivered, and by the time Christmas arrived he had saved enough money to buy a swell present for the whole family.

Chapter 7

Christmas 1943

Billy was almost as excited about Christmas as when he was a little kid. Danny could not understand that.

"Christmas ain't no big deal," he said.

"It is at our house," Billy said. "Ever since the war started my dad's been in work, so now we can afford Christmas. I remember when I was five years old, we only had a puny chicken my Aunt Aggie sent down from Muskoka. We didn't even know what a turkey looked like. And Bea says the year I was born they didn't even have a tree. Do you want to come to our house for Christmas, Hawk?"

"What'll your old man say?"

"I dunno. I'll find out."

So Billy asked his parents and his father

surprised him by saying, "That might be nice, what with Arthur away."

And his mother added, "Yas! The more the merrier."

* * *

On Christmas morning Billy was the first awake, as usual. The instant he realized what day it was, the old familiar thrill ran through him. He glanced at Jakey beside him and decided his brother wouldn't appreciate being awakened at dawn, no matter what day it was, so he quietly slipped out of bed.

As soon as his feet hit the cold linoleum floor, icy shivers snaked up his legs. He quickly pulled on his slippers and then crept down the hall to Bea's room. The door was shut, so he tapped lightly.

"You awake, Bea-Bea?"

"I'm coming, Billy!"

He could always count on Bea to join him for Christmas morning.

His parents appeared at their bedroom door in the semi-darkness, tying their kimono strings. Billy led the parade down the stairs in his striped pyjamas.

The Christmas tree shimmered in the pale morning light.

And there beside it, leaning against the armchair, was a shiny black Victory bike.

"Holy cow!" cried Billy in delight. He raced over to the bike, flung one long leg over the bar, grasped the leather handle grips and began to bounce on the black leather saddle.

"Now will you help me learn how to ride, Bea?"

"Sure, Billy. The first nice spring day," she promised.

"Thanks, Mum. Thanks, Dad. It's exactly what I wanted."

"Well, I hope you're not disappointed because it's not brand new," his father apologized.

"For land's sake, Jim, he never would have noticed if you hadn't drawn his attention to it," snapped his wife, irritably.

"Yes, I would," Billy said. "But that's okay. It's just as good as new."

He tested the bell with his thumb, shattering the silence and making everybody jump.

"I think I like it better than new."

He was determined to keep his parents in a happy mood for Christmas Day, especially since Danny was coming.

* * *

In the afternoon, he and Danny wandered along Bloor Street to kill time. Billy was disappointed that his father wouldn't allow him to take his bike out because of the snow.

"It's really a terrific bike, even if it isn't brand new. Wait'll you see it. What did you get, Hawk?"

"I don't know. My old lady didn't get our stuff wrapped up yet. We'll probably get something tomorrow."

Billy thought that was weird, but he didn't say so.

They stopped in front of the White Spot hamburger joint to admire the war poster in the window. It was a picture of a Canadian soldier in a steel helmet about to throw a hand grenade. Under it was the caption: BUY VICTORY BONDS!

The smell of frying onion drew them in the open door. Danny ordered two hamburgers to go.

"I don't want one," protested Billy. "I never eat all day on Christmas Day. I save up for dinner. My mum will be mad if we're not hungry, Hawk."

"I'll be hungry, Stretch, don't worry." Danny paid ten cents each for the hamburgers and began munching, first one, and then the other.

Back on the street they continued their trek. They passed airmen and sailors and soldiers, home on Christmas leave, their girlfriends clinging proudly to their arms.

Every once in a while Danny stopped, let out a loud belch and rubbed his stomach.

* * *

When they opened the kitchen door of Billy's house, the boys immediately smelled a delicious aroma. Fran Thomson had the roasting pan on the oven door and was basting the golden brown bird. When she was done, she pinched one of the drumsticks.

"The turkey-lurkey's almost done," she declared, easing the pan back into the oven.

Her cheeks were flushed from the heat and her dark hair clung in damp kiss-curls to her forehead.

"Merry Christmas, Danny," she said with a welcoming smile.

"Merry Christmas, Mrs. Thomson."

"Introduce your friend to the rest of the family, Billy, and show him the tree."

Danny stared around at the decorations. Red and green streamers looped across the ceiling from corner to corner and in the centre, where they came together, hung a white paper foldout bell. He gave a little whistle.

Billy made the introductions self-consciously.

"This here's Hawk . . . I mean Danny Thunder," he said.

Danny already knew Jakey, so they just eyed each other warily. Willa and her husband Clifford said a polite, "Merry Christmas," and, much to Billy's relief, Mr. Thomson took his new pipe out of his mouth and wished Danny a merry Christmas too.

Bea, who had been going around with a long face all day because she missed Lorne, perked right up.

"Oh, what big brown eyes you have!" she teased Danny, and his olive-brown complexion almost turned red.

A few minutes later, they all sat at the dining room table, which was set with Mrs. Thomson's best china. A bright red candle sat in a wreath of holly in the middle of the pure white cloth.

It looks like a cardinal nesting in the snow, Billy thought.

Mr. Thomson gave Billy and his guest each a drumstick and Jakey didn't even blink. Then, when everyone else had been served their choice of meat, the steaming bowls were passed around: fluffy mashed potatoes, savoury bread dressing, green and yellow vegetables, rich brown gravy swimming in a boat.

Danny picked up his fork and was about to dig in when Fran Thomson said, "Danny, would you like to say grace?"

Danny shot Billy a puzzled look and Billy understood.

"I'll say it," he said. Then they all bowed their heads and Billy muttered, "Lord, make us thankful for what we are about to receive. Amen."

When they were on their second helping, Fran said, "Be sure to save room for plum pudding!"

Danny stifled a groan and Billy said out of the side of his mouth, "I told you not to eat those hamburgers, Hawk."

The moist dark pudding was only part of the traditional dessert. Next came Fran's masterpiece, a fruit cake with almond icing dotted with tiny silver balls.

"It would kill a man twice to eat one slice of Mrs. Thomson's Christmas cake," sang Fran.

Everybody laughed and Billy explained to Danny, "Mum sings that every year and nobody's died yet."

* * *

After dinner, when the dishes were done, the family gathered in the front room to listen to "Scrooge's Christmas" on the Philco.

While the radio tubes were warming up, Fran Thomson said, "This might be a good time to show your friend the Christmas box you gave to the whole house, Bingo."

Willa jumped up and stood beside the light switch. "Tell me when," she said.

Billy got down on the floor, stretched himself out full length, and wriggled under the bottom branches of the spruce tree.

"WHEN!" he cried.

And then the magic happened: at the precise moment that the ceiling lights flashed off, coloured tree lights flashed on.

"Ohhh!" came the hushed whisper as the lights reflected in the glass balls, glittered on the tinsel icicles and sparkled in their shining eyes.

Danny had contrived to sit next to Bea on the wine velour chesterfield. Inclining her head towards him, she whispered, "Squint your peepers and you'll see twice as many lights."

So he squinted and sure enough he saw double.

"Wow!" he whispered back.

Billy stood beside his mother feeling as proud as punch of himself.

"It's beautiful, Bingo," she breathed. "I never thought I'd live to see the day when we'd have electric lights on our tree."

Then she gave him a sudden, bone-cracking hug and, instead of pulling away as he usually did, Billy hugged her back.

When the radio program was over, Billy and Danny put their outdoor clothes on.

"Thanks for the swell supper, Mrs. Thomson," Danny said.

"You're as welcome as the flowers in May," Fran Thomson laughed, and Billy could tell that his mum had taken a real shine to Danny. "Now just a tick, I've got something for your mother."

The famous fruitcake (which would kill a man twice) was sitting on the shelf of the kitchen cabinet covered with a damp tea towel to keep it moist. Mrs. Thomson removed the towel, cut a thick wedge, wrapped it in waxed paper, and handed it to Danny.

"Be sure to tell your mother to save it for New

Year's Eve so she'll have good luck all year long," she said, and a shadow crossed her face. "I hope the new year brings peace," she murmured, and Billy knew that she was thinking of Arthur again.

* * *

The boys arrived at the flat above the Cut-Rate at eight o'clock and all they could smell was roasting popcorn instead of turkey.

Aussie was shaking a huge iron skillet over the blue flame of the gas burner. Suddenly the lid of the skillet leapt in the air and white kernels flew all over the kitchen. Ralphie and Bevan caught them in mid-flight and popped them into their mouths.

"They're not for eating, you greedy sods!" cried their exasperated mother. "They're for stringing on the tree."

"But we're starving," moaned the boys.

"Oh, quit your bellyaching!" bellowed Mrs. Thunder.

"Bellyaching! Bellyaching!" mocked the saucy parrot.

"Shut up, Angel!" yelled the family with one voice.

Mrs. Thunder opened the oven door and poked a fork into a huge white turkey. She shut the door and turned the gas up.

"I forgot to put it in on time," she shrugged, "so what can you do?"

The boys glared at her with accusing, hungry eyes.

"Oh, go ahead then. Make pigs of yourselves. But you'll have to pop some more for the tree. Give some to Billy and Danny, too."

"Gee, thanks just the same, Mrs. Thunder, but I'm still stuffed from dinner," Billy apologized.

"Yeah, me too," Danny agreed, rubbing his stomach.

"Here, Ma. Mrs. Thomson sent you this for good luck. But you ain't supposed to eat it until New Year's Eve or you'll ruin the luck."

Just as Mrs. Thunder was opening the wax paper package, Mr. Thunder came in with a brown bag under his arm, twisted at the top. Holding the cake up to her nose, Mrs. Thunder sniffed appreciatively.

"What a sweet lady your mother is," she said to Billy. Then, blithely ignoring the good luck advice, she added, "I think I'll have a slice with a drinkie-poo to tide me over. What about you, Elwood?"

"Don't mind if I do, Snookey. The drinks are on me."

He untwisted the top of the bag and drew out a corked green bottle.

"Business is booming today," he chuckled as he pulled the cork out with his teeth. "Rationing this stuff is sure good for business."

He filled two tumblers with sparkling, amber-coloured liquid.

Settling on the couch in front of the picture window, he took a big bite of the fruitcake and washed it down with a long draught from his glass.

"Ahhh!" he sighed contentedly. "This here's the life. Tell your ma thanks a million, Skinny."

Billy beamed at the praise and hoped the Thunders wouldn't run into bad luck in the new year.

Looking around, Billy suddenly noticed a big, bushy evergreen propped up in a corner. But there was something missing — ornaments.

"Can I help decorate your tree, Mrs. Thunder?" he asked. "I'm good at it. I do it at our house."

"It's nice of you to offer, Peaches, but ever since we moved I've never been able to find the blasted box of decorations. The boys will just have to throw some popcorn on it."

And that's exactly what they did. Aussie popped another huge batch and, after eating their fill, they threw what remained on by the handful. The little white clouds clung all over the branches and Billy was surprised at how pretty it looked — like a tree in a snowstorm.

When that was done, Billy turned to Bevan.

"What did Santa Claus bring you, Bev?" he asked amiably.

"Are you nuts?" sneered the eight-year-old.

"We got Monopoly," Aussie said. "Antway, otay, laypay?"

"Huresay!"

Billy was pleasantly surprised by Aussie's

friendliness. He guessed it must be the Christmas spirit. But he soon realized that Aussie had an ulterior motive.

"You ever played before?" asked Aussie cagily.

"No, but I can learn."

Billy was instantly on guard.

"You got any money?"

"I've got a quarter."

"Two bits is better than a kick," Aussie said as he opened the board on the table.

The Thunders were a betting bunch. They never played for fun. So they each put up a quarter.

Ralphie was counting the play money and Billy could tell by the wrinkly bills that the Thunder boys had been practising.

Even though the game was new to him, it didn't take long for Billy to catch on. As his mother often remarked, he was sharp as a tack where money was concerned. Even play money.

In no time Billy controlled the board.

"I think I'll go into real estate when I grow up," he laughed as he took possession of Park Place and the Boardwalk. Then he erected hotels on both properties and bought the Railroads. In short order he swept the board clean and gathered up all the money.

Suddenly he noticed an ominous hush around the table. All the boys were glowering at him, including Danny. So he promptly threw the next two games and let them all break even.

By this time Aussie and Ralphie were groaning with hunger and Bevan had begun to cry.

Billy glanced up at the clock. It was 10:30.

"Gosh, I'd better phone my mother," he said.

"You do that, Peaches," Mrs. Thunder agreed as she relaxed on the couch and lit up a cigar.

Just then her husband came down the hall from the bathroom.

"You into my stogies again, Snookey? They're expensive Cubans you know."

"So! If they're good enough for you, they're good enough for me," she retorted, blowing out a thick grey cloud.

The smoke drifted in Angel's direction and he began coughing and gasping and finally collapsed with a crash upside down on the bottom of the cage. He lay perfectly still with his eyes shut and his feet sticking up.

"Oh, no! Angel!" Billy screamed.

But Mrs. Thunder just laughed and gave the cage a shake. "Get up on your spar, you phony old fowl," she said. "I'm on to your tricks."

Much to Billy's relief, Angel opened one eye, flopped over and hopped onto his spar, muttering and preening himself.

Mrs. Thunder handed the stogie to her husband and checked the turkey. It was gradually turning from opalescent white to translucent yellow.

"This monster won't be done for a dog's age," she

complained. "Some bonus! Cut-Rate should have given me a nicer one."

This news sent Bevan into a tantrum.

"There, there, Skeeter." His mother gave him an affectionate hug. "Go pick a bit of popcorn off the tree."

Then she said to Billy, who was dialling the phone, "You better tell your mother I said you can bunk over on the couch, Peaches."

Billy was thrilled at the invitation and immediately relayed it to his mother, who had just answered his ring.

"You mean to say they haven't had their Christmas dinner yet?" Fran Thomson shrieked.

Billy screwed the receiver into his ear and faced the wall to try to contain his mother's shrill voice.

"No. Not yet. Can I stay, Mum?"

"I'll ask your father."

"No. Just say yes. Please, Mum?"

There was a long pause and Billy could tell by the dead silence behind him that the whole Thunder clan, including Angel, was all ears.

Finally his mother spoke, "Oh, pshaw, what's the odds? Just you behave yourself so Violet will know you come from a good home. Did Danny give her my cake? And did he tell her to save it till New Year's?"

"He did, Mum. She says thanks. Bye, Mum." He hung up before she could change her mind.

* * *

At two o'clock in the morning, Mr. Thunder blew up.

"Tarnation, Snookey, we're going to eat that damn gobbler even if it's still clucking."

The boys, who were lying around snoozing, sprang to life and scrambled to their places at the picnic table.

Mr. Thunder rescued the sorry bird from the oven and proceeded to carve the half raw, half-blackened turkey while his wife dished up burned boiled potatoes, soggy dressing and mushy pork-and-beans.

Billy did his best to eat some of the unappetizing meal, but Danny didn't even try. His face had drained of colour and he was massaging his stomach in circles.

Suddenly Mr. Thunder stood up and his chair went tumbling backwards.

Raising his glass high, he thundered, "Merry Christmas to all, and to all a good night!"

Then he swallowed his drink in one gulp and disappeared down the hallway.

"And God bless us, every one," added Mrs. Thunder.

"God bless us, every one!" squawked Angel.

The next day they all slept in until two in the afternoon.

* * *

On their way down Durie Street, Billy said, "You're lucky you have so much fun at your house, Hawk. I never had Christmas dinner in the middle of the night before."

Danny shot Billy a suspicious glance through narrowed coal-black eyes.

"You mean it, Stretch?" he asked.

"Sure I mean it. I always have a swell time at your place."

"Yeah, well . . . " Danny hunched his shoulders and stuffed his fists deep into his pockets. "I never had Christmas dinner at dinner time before. Your Ma's a great cook, Stretch." Then, keeping his eyes on the ground, he added, "I like your whole family. 'Specially your sister Bea. It must be fun to have sisters."

Billy turned and caught Danny blushing. Hooting with laughter Billy poked Danny playfully in the ribs and cried, "Have you got a crush on Bea, Hawk? Oh, boy, wait'll I tell her."

"You do," Danny said with a ferocious scowl, "and you can kiss the world goodbye."

Then he began to give a hoarse laugh, which all at once changed into a piercing cry.

Grabbing his side, Danny spun around and collapsed into a snowbank.

At first Billy thought Danny was just fooling around, but when Danny remained curled in a tight ball in the snow, moaning softly to himself, Billy got scared.

"C'mon, Hawk. Get up!" urged Billy.

But Danny did not move, and suddenly Billy knew Danny was not fooling. He ran like the wind for help.

Chapter 8

Drop Dead

Danny nearly died of a ruptured appendix.

"Violet Thunder told me that the doctor at Saint Joseph's Hospital said if that boy wasn't as tough as shoe leather he never would have pulled through," Fran Thomson told her family the next night at the supper table.

"Poor little kid," remarked Bea, helping herself to the turkey stew and passing the bowl along to Billy. "I hope he'll be all right soon."

"It's still touch and go," her mother said. "He's not out of the woods yet. The poison raced all through his body and it'll take time for it to work its way out of his system."

"When can I go see him, Mum?" mumbled Billy.

"Don't talk with your mouth full, Bingo. I can't

say for sure. Why don't you run up to see his mother tomorrow? And while you're at it, ask her what nice treat I could make him."

Mrs. Thunder wasn't home when Billy called. She was at the hospital visiting Danny. And the boys were none too friendly, so Billy left by the back way.

The Chinese laundryman stared at him suspiciously, his mouth full of clothespegs. As Billy glanced away self-consciously, his eyes lit on the cellar window.

Through the muddy pane of glass he could just make out the shadowy figure of Mr. Thunder. But he didn't dare knock on the window because Danny had warned him never to let his old man catch him spying. Instead, Billy decided to phone Mrs. Thunder that night.

"Hi, Mrs. Thunder. It's me, Billy Thomson. How's Hawk . . . I mean how's Danny doing?"

"He's still a very sick boy." Billy had never heard Mrs. Thunder sound so serious before. "But the doctors say he's going to pull through." Then she added with a little chuckle, "It would take more than a busted appendix to kill my Danny-boy. Just as soon as he's fit for company I'll take you down to see him, Peaches."

"That'll be swell, Mrs. Thunder. And my mum wants to know what nice thing she can make him to eat."

"Ah, your mum's a sweetie. Tell her he likes butter tarts, but he won't be able to stomach them for a while."

"Okay, Mrs. Thunder. Tell Hawk I said 'Hi.' Bye."

Danny had to stay in the hospital two full weeks. Mrs. Thunder took Billy to see him halfway through the second week.

"By the way, how old are you, Billy?" she asked as they stepped off the Queen streetcar near Saint Joseph's.

"I'm eleven. Why?"

"Well, you're supposed to be twelve to get in the hospital. I'll say you're fourteen for good measure."

Billy had never been inside a hospital before, not even when he was born, since he was born at home. The mediciney smells wafting down the corridors made him feel queasy, so he tried to take his mind off it by gawking into all the rooms. And that's how he found Danny.

Danny was proud as punch of his stitches. And he was bound and determined to show them off. So he gritted his teeth and ripped the adhesive bandage down one side, revealing a long crooked ladder on his abdomen.

"Take a gander, Stretch! You ever seen anything like that before? Go ahead, count them."

The gory scar and the bloodstained bandage made Billy turn his head and retch. But he swallowed hard and obligingly counted twenty-four black, knotted stitches.

* * *

Danny came home on the first day of school in 1944, but the doctor refused him permission to attend classes for two more weeks, or until the stitches came out. Danny said the holiday was worth nearly dying for.

Billy found himself at loose ends. So one day he decided to call on Sammy Watson. He had been ignoring Sammy ever since Danny had become his best buddy, and he felt sort of bad about it. After all, Sammy couldn't help the fact that he was dumb and boring.

He approached the Watsons' house quietly because of the sign tacked to the door. On it was a picture of a little girl with her finger to her lips, saying, "Shhh! A War Worker Is Sleeping!"

Mr. Watson was on the night shift making Mosquito aircraft at DeHavilland.

Billy tapped very lightly. Sammy opened the door.

"Hi, Sam. Ready for school?" Billy asked.

"Drop dead!" snapped Sammy, and he slammed the door so hard the sign flapped wildly in Billy's face.

Billy's heart dropped like a stone and he made his way dejectedly to school.

Right after "God Save the King" and "Rule Britannia," Sammy put his hand up.

The Owl ignored him and began reading a poem

PLEASE!

A WAR WORKER IS SLEEPING

by Edgar Guest: "It was indeed an evil hour, when Adolph Hitler came to power . . . "

Sammy waved his hand so persistently that Mr. Little stopped in mid-poem and barked, "Well, Watson, can't you wait until recess?"

The class snickered and made hissing noises.

"Please, sir. I want to move my seat," Sammy said.

"What for?"

Sammy glared at Billy. "Something stinks here," he said.

The Owl's tufted eyebrows rose above his horn-rimmed glasses.

"Well, move!" he snapped impatiently. "Take that empty seat in the third row. Now where was I?"

The class reminded him where he was and Sammy made a big show of moving.

Billy felt both hurt and guilty, so he tried to think of ways to make up with Sammy. But he didn't realize how mad Sammy was until recess. It was then he discovered that Sammy had joined Rock Hammer's gang.

They were all grouped together in the far corner of the schoolyard. And in the middle of the tight circle stood their leader.

Billy kept his distance and watched them out of the corner of his eye as he scooped up a handful of snow and patted it into a smooth ball, pretending disinterest in what the gang was up to.

But despite himself, he felt his stomach muscles tighten nervously, so he sauntered toward another group of boys who were tossing snowballs over the fence at a bunch of laughing girls.

Billy joined in the fun, turning his back on the gang.

Suddenly, like a bolt from the blue, something hard slammed into the back of his head, knocking his tuque off. For a second the world reeled around him. Shaking his head, he bent down for his hat. Beside it lay the remains of the snowball that had hit him. In the centre of the shattered missile was a stone the size of a golf ball.

He was just straightening up, his head still spinning, when Rock Hammer charged into him, taking him to the ground and knocking the wind out of him.

Rock knelt over Billy, his green eyes glittering viciously. "Whatcha gonna do without the Mohawk, Baby-Bo Bango?" he hissed, spitting expertly, right in his victim's eye.

The insult made Billy lash out with all his might.

Infuriated, Rock yelled at his gang, "You guys hold him down!" and the boys jumped to obey, pinning Billy to the ground. This left Rock's fists free to mercilessly pummel Billy's face.

By the time a teacher came running to the rescue, Billy's face had been beaten to pulp.

Willing hands helped him into the school and eased him onto the couch in the nurse's office.

The nurse felt his swollen, bloody nose gingerly. "You're lucky it isn't broken," she said.

Then she cleaned him up and put a patch on his blacker eye.

"You'd better go straight home and have your mother take you to the dentist," she advised. "That front tooth looks loose to me."

Fran Thomson was just struggling up the cellar stairs with the wash basket when Billy came limping in the door like a wounded soldier.

"Merciful heavens! What happened to you?" she cried, the basket falling from her hands, wet clothes spilling on the floor.

"Rock Hammer beat me up," Billy mumbled through split and bloody lips. "The nurse says my tooth might be loose."

Mrs. Thomson carefully tried to wiggle his front tooth. "I think it's all right, but sakes alive, Bingo, why does that ruffian pick on you? What did you do?"

"I didn't do anything," he insisted, gagging on his own blood. "Rock Hammer is just a bully, is all."

"I'm going straight to the principal about him," declared his mother.

"No, Mum. Don't do that, or he'll murder me next time."

"Well, you go straight to bed now and I'll be right up."

Mrs. Thomson took a hand towel outside and packed it with snow, then she followed Billy upstairs and placed the compress gently on his swollen cheek.

"You try to sleep now, love. I have to get those clothes hung on the line while the sun's shining or they'll never dry. Then I'll make you a nice poached egg on toast."

Ever since the gnawing hunger of the depression years, Fran Thomson thought that good food was a cure-all for whatever ailed you.

Soothed by the cool snow pack and his mother's sympathy, Billy let himself drift into a daydream. He began to wonder . . . was Sammy one of the guys that held him down? Or was he the one who ran to get the teacher and then helped him into the nurse's office? He could not remember.

Chapter 9

The Meat Market

"Can I go up to see Hawk today, Mum? Mrs. Thunder said I could."

Nearly a week had passed since the big fight and Billy felt and looked a lot better.

"I guess so. But steer clear of that beastly bully."

"Don't worry, Mum. I only see Rock at school. And besides it's Saturday and he always has to help his dad at the brick works on Saturdays."

"Thank goodness for small blessings," sighed his mother. "And since you're going to the meat market, you might as well get my blade roast for Sunday supper."

Hopping up on the little stool that enabled her to reach the top of the kitchen cabinet, Fran Thomson got down her pocketbook, unsnapped it and drew out two one-dollar bills.

"Now don't lose it. Money doesn't grow on trees you know. And be sure to bring back my change."

Promising to be careful, Billy set off up Veeny Street. Just as he reached the corner he saw Ernst Vierkoetter come bounding out of his house and down the front steps.

"Hi, Mr. Vierkoetter!" cried Billy.

"Hello there, Bill!"

Ernst Vierkoetter was Billy's hero. He knew by heart the story of how he had won the first-ever Wrigley marathon swim held at the Canadian National Exhibition in 1927.

It had been a gruelling twenty-one miles in the bitter cold waters of Lake Ontario. Ernst Vierkoetter had been the only man to finish, and when they helped him out at the end, he was covered in bloodsucking eels. But it had been worth it because he became known as the Black Shark of Germany and was crowned champion of the world. And the grand prize was a fortune: $30,000!

Billy also knew that a lot of World War One veterans, including his own dad, had been mad as hops about a German winning all that good Canadian cash. But his mother declared that any man who had braved eleven hours in 44-degree water deserved every cent he got.

"Are you going to sign up for swimming lessons again this year, Bill?" asked the great marathoner.

"Sure, Mr. Vierkoetter. Are you going to be our coach again?"

"You bet. And I expect you to be my champion this year, Bill." He pulled keys out of his pocket.

"Like you, Mr. Vierkoetter," beamed Billy.

The big man laughed, ducked his head and climbed into his 1943 Packard.

"Goodbye then, young Bill. See you at the swimming tank!"

He honked the horn and sped away.

Billy continued up the street, walking on a cloud. Mr. Vierkoetter's words made him feel good. Swimming was the only sport he excelled in. He had won top honours in the junior and intermediate classes, and now he would be going for his senior's badge. He wished Hawk could see him swim. Maybe he should ask him if he wanted to sign up too.

Turning onto Durie Street, he noticed the indentation in the snowbank where Danny had fallen. Some of the snow had melted in the January thaw, but the outline of Danny's curled-up body could still be made out. For a reason that he didn't understand, the shape in the snow made him mad, so he stamped on it until it was completely obliterated.

He decided to buy his mother's blade roast first, so he went around to the Bloor Street door. There was a new poster in the meat market window. It was a coloured picture of a housewife filling a tin can with drippings from her frying pan. Under it were the words: "Canada needs forty million pounds of fat to make glycerine. Glycerine makes bombs to fry Berlin!" Gee, Billy thought, I'd better tell Mum about that.

The bell over the door jangled as he went in. There was a lineup at Mrs. Thunder's wicket, so she didn't see Billy at first. But when she looked up to give her customer change, their eyes met and she gave him a big smile and a wink.

Billy returned Mrs. Thunder's smile, but he could see that she was too busy to talk, so he went to the meat counter and waited his turn. Gathering a pile of sawdust between his rubber boots, he examined the trays of meat in the long, glass case: layers of butterfly pork chops, piles of pink sausages, mounds of hamburger, hams and pork hocks, thick curled ox tongues and glistening slabs of wine-coloured liver.

The gory display made his stomach heave, so he quickly slid sideways, making a path through the sawdust to the end of the counter. The last tray was loaded with thick, juicy T-bone steaks. Billy recognized them because he'd eaten them once.

It had been his first Sunday dinner at Danny's. Mrs. Thunder had fast fried T-bone steaks with chopped onions and garlic in sizzling brown butter. Great clouds of smoke had filled the kitchen, so Mr. Thunder had flung open the window onto Bloor Street. Billy had hung out the window to get fresh air and the people waiting at the streetcar stop had craned their necks, sniffing the smoke.

One man in a fedora had hollered up, "What's cooking?" and Billy had hollered back, "Steaks!" and the man had cried, "Lucky you! Bon appetit!" as he ran for the streetcar.

The steaks were the most delicious meat Billy had ever tasted, black on the outside and pink on the inside. The thought of them filled his mouth with water.

"What'll it be, kid? I haven't got all day."

Billy jumped and swallowed and the butcher guffawed. Then he wiped his bloody hands down the bib of his apron and Billy noticed that his left little finger was missing.

It reminded him of the story Bea told about the butcher who had accidentally ground up his finger in the hamburger machine. The man had sworn by all that was good and holy that he'd thrown that batch of hamburger into the garbage can. But nobody knew for sure.

Mesmerized by the missing finger, Billy hesitated too long and the butcher turned to his next customer. So when his turn came again, he waved the two bills importantly and asked, "How many T-bones can I get for this, mister?"

"Mr. Wiener to you, kid," the man said, and Billy didn't know if he was joking or not. He flopped two steaks on the scales and said, "That's it, kid."

Billy knew it wasn't nearly enough meat for the

whole family, and that his mother would be mad as hops, but he could see that Mr. Wiener was losing his patience, so he said, "I'll take them."

Mr. Weiner wrapped the steaks in shiny brown butchers' paper, tied the package with a string that dangled from a spool above his head, took a pencil stub from behind his ear and wrote $2.00 on the package.

There was still a long lineup at the wicket, so while Billy waited, he amused himself by counting the seconds off on the big round clock on the wall. He could actually see the seconds slipping by through a little round hole above the six.

His mother always said that the Cut-Rate clock gave her the willies because it was like watching her life sliding by before her very eyes. It gave her the same weird feeling, she said, as if someone had just walked over her grave.

"Penny for your thoughts, Peaches!"

Billy had moved up in the line automatically without realizing it.

Taking a closer look, Mrs. Thunder exclaimed, "Where in tarnation did you get that shiner?"

Billy felt his eye gingerly.

"I got it in a fight," he said with a touch of pride.

"Well, ain't you a pip! Pretty soon you'll be as bad as my boys," she chuckled.

"What's that you got there?"

"They're T-bone steaks."

"Well, be sure and tell your mother to put one on your eye before she fries it. Works every time."

"Okay, Mrs. Thunder."

Billy slid the money and the ration book through the slot under the window.

Violet Thunder darted a secretive look in the direction of the two butchers. Billy furtively followed her glance. One man was cheerfully cleaving off turkey heads on the scarred wooden chopping block. Mr. Weiner was busy at the scales, weighing his thumb along with a mound of hamburger. There was no one else waiting in line.

Leaning forward, her red lips almost touching the round hole in the glass partition, Mrs. Thunder whispered, "Put your money away and skite up the stairs, Peaches."

"Gee, thanks, Mrs. Thunder," Billy whispered back. Then he stuffed the money and ration book inside his windbreaker and headed for the stairs at the back of the store.

Grinning to himself as he made his way up the dark stairwell, he thought, Mum can't be mad about the steaks if they didn't cost anything. Not even a ration coupon.

Chapter 10

Return of the Hawk

Danny was lying on his back on the couch, balancing a barbell over his head. Despite his dark skin, he looked pale and thin. His straight black hair was fanned out from his face on a white pillow. It made his high cheekbones stand out like chicken wings.

Danny lowered the barbell to his chest and then heaved it with a grunt to the floor. Then, clutching his side, he eased himself into a sitting position.

"How're you doing, Hawk?" Billy asked.

Instead of answering, Danny surveyed his friend with narrowed eyes and asked, "What happened to you, Stretch?"

"Aw, this is nothing." Billy touched his discoloured eye. "You should have seen it on Monday. It was black as coal. And the school nurse thought my nose was broken and my front tooth was loose."

"Were you in an accident?"

"No. I had a fight with Rock Hammer. And guess what else? Sammy Watson's joined his gang."

Danny's black eyes flashed with anger. "Pickin' on you is the same as pickin' on me. But, don't worry, Stretch. When I get back to school, I'll take care of both of them."

"Heck, no, Hawk. I can take care of myself."

"Sure you can. That's how come you look like you just got back from the war."

Danny hoisted the barbell up off the floor, lay back on the couch and started exercising again.

"Just give me a week," he said.

Billy knew better than to argue with him, but he wished, just for once, that Hawk would mind his own business.

"Where did you get that thing?" he asked, just to change the subject.

"Seven . . . eight . . . nine . . . ten!"

With a loud huff, Danny dropped the weight with a thud to the floor.

"It ain't a 'thing.' It's a barbell. My old man won it off Popeye Parker in a crap game. Popeye used to be a pugilist."

"What's a pugilist?"

"Geez, Stretch, how dumb can you get? Don't you read Joe Palooka?"

"Sometimes. But I like books better than comics.

I've read five books since Monday 'cause my mother kept me home. I just finished *Hound of the Baskervilles* by Arthur Conan Doyle. It's real scary. Want me to tell you about it?"

"You do and your name's mud. Books won't help you beat up guys like Rock Hammer, for pete's sake."

Danny rolled the barbell towards Billy with his foot and said, "Pick it up."

Billy put the butcher's parcel on the table, then he bent over at the waist and grabbed the barbell.

"No! Not like that. You'll bust your back. Bend your knees and keep your back straight."

Following Danny's instructions, Billy managed to lift the weight a little ways off the floor before letting it drop with a crash.

Danny snorted triumphantly.

"See what I mean, Stretch? You're the brains and I'm the brawn, and don't you forget it!"

Billy felt the hair on the back of his neck rise at Danny's words, but he bit his tongue and didn't answer. Instead, he reminded himself that Danny made a better friend than an enemy.

"This exercising makes a guy thirsty," Danny said. "Get a couple of bottles of pop out of the refrigerator, Stretch."

The Thunders always had cold pop in their electric refrigerator. The Thomsons only had an icebox, and Billy's mother only bought ice in the summer. In winter she kept the milk and butter in the milk box by the back door. When the temperature dipped below freezing, the cream on top of the bottle turned to ice and pushed the lid up. Sometimes Jakey and Billy would fight over the frozen cream, as fiercely as if it was a popsicle.

They had just finished guzzling down the last two bottles of Kik Cola when they heard Danny's brothers coming up the back stairs. Quick as a wink, Danny rolled the empty bottles under the couch.

The first thing the three boys did was make a dash for the refrigerator.

"Who drank all the pop?" demanded Aussie, darting Billy a dirty look.

"I did," Danny said. "Wanna make something of it?"

Even in Hawk's weakened condition, his big brother backed down.

Billy hurriedly took his leave.

"So long, Hawk. I'll be seeing you," he said, and bolted down the stairs.

Yep, he decided to himself, I better keep Danny for my best friend.

When his mother cut the string and unwrapped the parcel of meat, she was fit to be tied.

"Where's my blade roast?" she demanded. "How am I supposed to feed seven people with these two scraps of meat? I'm not a magician you know!"

Billy just grinned and gave her back the two dollars and the ration book with no coupons missing.

"Oh, my!" Mrs. Thomson gasped excitedly. "This looks like Violet Thunder's doing."

She hopped up on the little stool and hid the money in the biscuit tin on top of the cabinet.

"That'll buy me my new Easter bonnet," she said, rubbing her hands together in her excited way. "I hope you remembered to thank Mrs. Thunder, Bingo."

"Yeah, I did, Mum."

Now she was examining the T-bone steaks. "How am I going to make these two morsels do," she puzzled. Then suddenly her face brightened. "I've got an idea . . . I'll chop them into stewing beef and stretch them out with gravy and dumplings."

"Aww, Mum, don't do that. You're supposed to fry them in butter with onion and garlic. That's what Mrs. Thunder does and it tastes swell."

"And stink my house up to high heaven? Not on your tintype. Anyhow, who's the best cook, me or Violet Thunder? Not that I'm speaking against her, mind. Everybody's got their faults."

Billy sighed and gave up on the steaks.

"You're the best cook, Mum," he reassured her.

"Well, I should say so. And how's Danny doing?"

"He's okay. He's lifting barbells to get strong again."

"Tsk! Tsk!" His mother shook her head in disbelief. "And to think only a few weeks ago he was at death's door. That boy is a Tartar, if there ever was one."

Billy scowled and went to deliver his Saturday papers.

Just for once, he thought, I wish Mum would call me a Tartar.

Chapter 11

The Lancaster

Another week went by and Billy began to miss Danny.

"Mum, can I ask Hawk for supper tonight?" he asked.

Fran Thomson was sitting at the kitchen table re-reading Arthur's latest letter for the umpteenth time.

"Mum . . ."

His mother glanced up impatiently. "What is it, Billy?"

"Can Hawk come for supper tonight."

"Is his appendix all better?"

"Yep. He's been exercising to build up his muscles. He says he can hardly wait to pick a fight with Rock Hammer."

"Well, if you want my opinion," his father shook the remnants of the coal scuttle into the stove and the coal dust sparked and crackled as it hit the fire, "that Thunder boy is nothing but a troublemaker. I don't think he gets proper training at home."

Ignoring this remark, Fran said, "I've got an idea." She folded Arthur's letter, slipped it into her apron pocket, and got the mixing bowl from the cupboard. "Since you overslept and missed church this morning, Bingo, maybe we can kill two birds with one stone. Why don't you take Danny to Sunday School with you this afternoon, and then you can bring him home for supper?"

"Aw, Mum. The Thunders don't go to church. I heard Mr. Thunder say he's an agnostic."

"Well, for land's sake, Billy, what's an agnostic? I've never heard of such a creature."

"I can tell you, Mum." Bea turned away from the little mirror above the kitchen sink where she had been putting on lipstick. "An agnostic is a person who doesn't know whether to believe in God or not."

"Well, I never . . . " Fran Thomson shook her head in dismay.

"If you want my opinion," Jim Thomson decided to try again, "I think you should go back to chumming with Sammy Watson. At least we know what kind of home he springs from."

"The Thunders have a swell home," protested Billy.

"You can't judge folks until you've walked a mile in their shoes," Fran philosophized. "That's what my father always said." She cracked two eggs on the side of the bowl, tipped them in, and began beating with a fork.

"Does that mean he can come, Mum?"

"Yas, I suppose so." She added a scoop of sugar and beat more vigorously.

Billy leaned over and sniffed the creamy mixture, "What are you making, Mum?"

"Banhanner pie, Bingo," she joked. Then her smile died on her face. "That's what Arthur always called banana-cream pie when he was a little gaffer," she sighed.

"I bet Hawk will like it," Billy said.

"Hmph!" snorted his father as he disappeared into the cellarway with the empty coal scuttle.

Billy headed for the telephone in the dining room. but Jakey had reached it first.

"Hurry, up. I gotta phone Hawk," Billy said.

Placing the flat of his hand over the bell-shaped mouthpiece that flared out of the hardwood phone box, Jakey growled, "Get lost, twerp."

"I don't hafta."

Billy flipped a chair around backwards and straddled it, hooking his toes behind the curved back legs.

"I said beat it," Jakey threatened.

"No!"

Suddenly Jakey removed his hand from the

mouthpiece and whispered, "I'll call you back, Bessie," and hung up.

Before Billy realized what was going to happen, he and the chair went crashing to the floor and Jakey was making a fast getaway upstairs.

"Oww!" hollered Billy, belatedly.

His mother came running from the kitchen, one hand cupped under the dripping fork.

"My stars, Billy, what are you doing down there? Are you hurt?"

"Nah, I'm okay. The chair just fell over is all."

He decided not to tell on Jakey in hopes that he wouldn't be mad about Danny coming for supper. Jakey didn't seem to like Hawk any more than his father did.

Untangling his long legs from the chair, he set it upright, limped over to the telephone and dialled Danny's number.

Danny answered.

"Hi, Hawk!" Billy decided to give him the good news first. "My mum says you can come to our house for supper tonight and she's making banana-cream pie."

"Sounds swell, Stretch. I never tasted it before."

"But there's one other thing." Billy paused so long that Danny got suspicious.

"Like what?"

"Like . . . well, we have to go to Sunday school this afternoon because I missed church this morning."

"Church!"

"No. Sunday school. It's not half as bad."

"Sunday school!"

"Yeah, well . . . aw, forget it, Hawk. I'll see you tomorrow."

This time there was a long pause on Danny's end of the line.

Billy was just about to hang up when Danny said, "Okay. I guess it won't kill me. What does a guy have to wear to church?"

"Just so long as you got on a tie."

"I'll borrow one of my old man's," Danny said, and hung up.

* * *

That night, as they sat around the dining room table, Fran Thomson asked Danny how he had enjoyed Sunday school.

"It ain't half bad," he said. "I kind of liked the music. That lady sure can play the piano."

"That was no lady, that was our cousin Ruth," Bea laughed. She always got a kick out of Danny. "Ruth's got perfect pitch," she added.

"I didn't know cousin Ruth was a good baseball player too," remarked Billy.

"Geez, you're stupid," Jakey sneered, still mad about his interrupted phone call.

"Yeah, well I'm not stupid enough to have Bessie

Beasley for a girlfriend," retorted Billy.

"Shut yer yap!"

"Shut yours!"

"One more word . . . " warned their father.

"Sounds just like home," Danny said, and made Bea laugh.

Billy noticed that Bea laughed a lot when Danny was around.

Mrs. Thomson came in from the kitchen carrying a pie that looked like a picture out of *Ladies Home Journal*.

"Do you like banhanner pie, Danny?" she asked, serving him the biggest slice.

"I never tasted it before, Mrs. Thomson. My old lady . . . I mean my mother . . . don't bake stuff. Mostly we have ice cream."

"Well, we don't have ice cream too often because it melts so fast in the icebox, but I sure do my share of baking. Try it and see how you like it."

Fran made everybody else wait while Danny took his first bite.

"Mmmm," he swallowed and licked the whipped cream off his lips. "It's the best pie I ever et."

Flushed with pride, Fran patted Danny's head affectionately — and Billy felt the sting of jealousy again.

When every crumb was gone and they were drinking their tea — the boys had water because kids under fourteen didn't get a tea-ration — Danny said to Bea, "Stretch told me your husband's in the air force, Bea. Is he a pilot?"

"No, he's a navigator," she answered proudly.

"What does a navigator do?"

"It's funny you should ask because I just got a letter from Lorne yesterday telling me what a navigator's job is all about. I didn't realize before that I didn't understand myself what a navigator does. I'll read it to you after supper if you like. It's really interesting because it got by the censors."

After Bea had helped with the washing-up, they all gathered in the small front room to listen to Lorne's letter.

Billy crossed his long legs and sat at Bea's feet. Hearing about Lorne's exploits always made him tremble with a mixture of excitement and fear. He wished he was brave, like Lorne, or tough, like Hawk.

"Somewhere in England," Bea began, her voice taking on an air of mystery. "January 3, 1944."

> *My dearest wife,*
>
> *I hope you had a happy new year. I can't tell you how much I miss you. Last night, I leaned across ten thousand miles to kiss you . . .*

"Ah, Booky!" the childish name slipped from her mother's lips.

Bea swallowed the lump in her throat and continued:

> *I keep your picture in my breast pocket next to my heart. All the boys carry snapshots for*

*good luck of their wives or girlfriends back
home, but none of them are as pretty as you.*

"Wow, Bea, you're blushing!" Danny teased, and
Billy wished he'd just shut up and listen.

"Just get on with it," barked Mr. Thomson. "You'd
think Lorne Huntley was the only boy who ever left
hearth and home for king and country."

"Yeah, and skip the mush," put in Jakey.

Bea gave them both a withering glance before she
continued.

*Last night was our crew's twentieth opera-
tion. Ten more and we'll have completed our
first tour of duty. The mission was a great
success, but a hair-raising experience.*

Bea shuddered and Danny said, "Don't read any
more if it bothers you, Bea."

"I'm all right," she assured him and read on.

*You asked in your last letter what a
navigator actually does, Bea, so I'll try to ex-
plain, but I'm not allowed to say too much.*

*First of all, a navigator's duty is to know the
precise location of his aircraft at all times.
There are different ways of doing this. We use
radar, radio and the sextant, and sometimes we
take our bearings from heavenly bodies such as
the moon and the stars, just like the ancient
mariners used to. But a navigator's most important job is to guide the pilot over the target at
exactly the right moment. We have to stay alert*

*throughout the entire operation so as to be
ready for Jerry's tricks. He's constantly trying
to confuse us with false signals and radio
beams. And of course there's always the danger
of being shot down over enemy territory.*

*Last night, for instance, we literally limped
home on a wing and a prayer. We were pretty
badly shot up, but not half as bad as Jerry. Our
gunner, Pete Kozak, who's my best buddy,
blasted a Messerschmitt right out of the sky at
300 yards, sending it down in a ball of flames.
Oh, what a beautiful sight that was!*

Bea drew in her breath and a pall of silence fell
over the room.

Then her mother whispered, "The Lord have
mercy on those poor German boys."

"Well, that's the way it is in wartime," Jim Thomson shrugged. "It's either them or you. I ought to
know. It was the same for us in France back in 1917."

Billy heard his mother mutter, "Oh, for pity
sakes!" under her breath. Mr. Thomson must have
made that same statement a million times before.

Bea continued,

*That's putting my job in a nutshell, darling.
And I hope I don't sound too boastful when I say
that as a good navigator, and the boys in my
crew tell me I'm the best, I'm the busiest fellow
in the plane.*

Actually, the fact is, all seven of our crew are

*the best in the business, maybe in the whole
RCAF.*

*And we all feel the same about our job. It's
the most exciting, exhilarating feeling in the
world to be hurtling through the black of night
with hundreds of other aircraft, each carrying
a deadly load of ten-ton bombs.*

*Now, if this letter slips by the censors, Bea, I
want you to promise me not to repeat a word of it.*

Remember, careless talk costs lives!

"How come I wonder?" asked Billy.

"I can answer that," Jim Thomson said. "I heard
tell of a soldier who told his sweetheart what troop
train he'd be on. Then she told her father, and he
talked at his workplace and was overheard by a spy.
Then the spy gave instructions to the saboteur to
wreck the troop train. And that's how the whole
platoon got wiped out."

"Did that really happen, Dad, or is it just Nazi
propaganda?" asked Jakey sceptically.

"It really happened, you can mark my words. But
that was in the first World War."

"Then we'll all have to promise not to breathe a
word," Fran Thomson said.

"You boys cross your hearts and swear," Bea said,
and the three boys spit on their hands and crossed
their hearts and swore.

Satisfied, she went on.

Now for some pleasanter news! Last week

*when Pete and I were on leave in London, we
saw King George inspecting a bomb site. Pete
got to shake his hand. I didn't get the chance,
but I was close enough to hear every word he
said, and he didn't stutter once.*

"Why would the king stutter?" asked Jakey.

"Because he's a famous stutterer, stupid.
Everybody knows that!" scoffed Billy, glad to give
Jakey his comeuppance.

They all waited for Bea to continue reading, but
she didn't. Instead she stared at the letter with a
worried expression on her face.

"What is it, Booky? What's the matter?" Fran
asked.

"I only hope Lorne steers clear of those English
girls in London," Bea said uneasily. "I've heard tell
they're terrible flirts, and they don't care if a fellow
is married or not. Wanda Backhouse's husband fell
in love with a WAC. He wrote home and asked for a
divorce. Wanda's mother said Wanda went completely hysterical and had to be taken to Dr. Smelly for
a shot. She doesn't think Wanda will ever get over
it."

"Oh, pshaw, Booky." Her mother leaned over and
squeezed her hand. "You don't need to worry about
your husband. Lorne is true-blue. And I never did
trust that Backhouse boy, anyways. He had a shifty
look about him, if you ask me."

"Gosh, Bea," Danny said, gazing at her with admiring eyes. "You don't have to worry about nobody being prettier than you."

"Oh, puke!" Jakey said, and for once Billy agreed with him.

"Why, thank you, Danny!" Bea said. Glaring at Jakey, she folded the letter and carefully slipped it back into its V-for-Victory envelope. "I think I'll go upstairs and answer it now. Goodnight, everyone. Goodnight, Danny-boy." And all of a sudden she leaned down and gave him a peck on the cheek.

Danny blushed and Billy scowled. Bea laughed as she ran off, clickety-click on her high heels up the stairs.

Jim Thomson switched the radio on and a minute later, after the tubes had warmed up, they heard Charlie McCarthy joking with Edgar Bergen in his funny, grating voice. It was one of the family's favourite programs, so they all settled back to listen.

But this time, after hearing the drama and excitement of Lorne's real-life wartime adventures, the jokes that came out of the mouth of the famous ventriloquist's dummy sounded as hollow as the dummy's wooden head.

Chapter 12

Good Riddance

The first thing The Owl did on Monday morning was to hand out new war savings books. Starting at the back of the classroom, he dropped one on every desk.

"As you know, each stamp costs twenty-five cents." Plop. "Sixteen stamps fill a book." Plop. "When you've stamped out Hitler's heinous face on every page, you may send your book to the following address: The National Chairman, War Savings Committee, On His Majesty's Service, Ottawa, Ontario." Plop.

"In due time you will receive a five-dollar war savings certificate." Plop. "Now that's what I call mixing good business with patriotism. While doing your share for the war effort, you will also be earning good dividends. If you don't know what that means, look it up." Plop. "Remember, each stamp buys twelve bullets." Plop. "Any questions?"

The last book landed on Danny's desk and he shot up his hand.

"Well, Thunder?"

"Where are we supposed to get the money from?"

"Earn it!" Mr. Little's voice rose with his tufted eyebrows. "Earn it by the sweat of your brow. Shovel snow. Mend fences. Mow lawns. Use elbow grease. Run errands. Earn it, boy. Just so long as you do not" — he wagged his finger in Danny's face — "and I repeat, DO NOT beg money from your parents. I'm sure they've already done their fair share to rid the world of the beast of Berlin. Now it's your turn. It's your bounden duty to come to the aid of the Empire.

"Rule Britannia! There'll always be an England!" he bellowed, thumping Danny's desk twice for emphasis.

Suddenly he tucked in his chin and glared down at Danny, his glasses sliding to the end of his nose. "By the way, Thunder, how are you feeling these days?" he asked.

"Fine," Danny answered. "How's yourself?"

Mr. Little gave one of his rare laughs. "I'm fine, too, Thunder. Glad to hear you're feeling better. Did you get the work done that I sent home with Thomson?"

"Some of it."

"Why not all of it?"

"Too sick," Danny said, and the sallow skin drawn tightly over his high cheekbones bore him out.

"Well, you do your utmost the rest of the year, and I'll keep your recent illness in mind," promised The Owl.

Danny arched one black eyebrow and exchanged an amazed glance with Billy.

"All right, class, enough of this shilly-shallying. Out with your work books."

Mr. Little's chalk began screeching a problem across the blackboard.

"If a Lancaster bomber flies 215 miles per hour, how long will it take to reach Berlin?"

"Hot dog!" Billy said under his breath. He loved math questions. Especially if they were about the war. He planned on joining the Air Force, if only the war lasted long enough. Then maybe his mother would worry about him all the time, just like she worried about Arthur.

He had pictures of Allied aircraft stuck all over his bedroom walls. His favourite was the Spitfire, known as the darling of the RAF.

He had persuaded his mother to buy only Canada cornstarch and Crown Brand corn syrup because the labels could be exchanged for free pictures. And his Aunt Milly, a dyed-in-the-wool Sweet Cap smoker, saved him the Air Spotter cards that came with every pack.

At recess, Danny surveyed the boys' side of the schoolyard with narrowed eyes.

"Where's Rock hiding out?" he growled.

Billy swept the schoolyard with a wide blue gaze.

"He must be away," he said. "And look, his gang is all split up. There's Sammy over there by himself. I'll go ask him."

Loping across the muddy yard, he stopped short beside his former friend. Sammy was throwing a baseball up in the air and catching it.

"Hi, Sam!"

Billy tried to sound extra friendly. Sammy just kept on throwing the ball and catching it.

"You seen Rock today?" Billy persisted.

"Who wants to know?"

"Me."

"What for?"

"No reason."

"Well, he ain't here."

Sammy turned suddenly and pitched the ball overhand to Buster Burton. Buster caught it and zinged it straight at Billy. By sheer luck, Billy caught it. A searing pain stung his hand. Gritting his teeth, he tossed the ball underhand to Sammy.

"Where is he?" he asked, rubbing his hands together.

Sammy dropped the ball between his feet and looked Billy straight in the eye.

"He moved," he said.

"Moved! What do you mean, moved?"

"Moved! Moved! You know. A truck backed up to

their front door and they piled all their stuff in and moved."

"Away?"

"Sure away."

"Away where?"

"How should I know?"

"Well, you're one of his gang, aren't you?"

Sammy did a quick little jump that made the ball spring up into his hands. Then he rolled it up one arm, over his shoulders, and down the other.

"Not really," he responded. "I just didn't know what else to do."

Billy felt a prick of conscience, but as luck would have it, he was saved by the bell.

"I'll see you later," he called over his shoulder as he made a mad dash to get behind Danny in line. They began marching to the ding, ding, ding of the bell.

"Hawk!"

"Yeah?"

"He moved. Rock Hammer moved."

"No kidding."

"That's what Sammy said."

"Lucky for him."

"Yeah. Good riddance to bad rubbish."

* * *

The Happy Gang was singing "There'll be Bluebirds Over the White Cliffs of Dover" on the radio when

Billy came home for lunch. His mother was whistling along with them as she stirred a pot of fragrant soup on the stove.

She gave Billy a taste from the spoon.

"Mmm, it's good, Mum," he said.

Putting a plate of soda biscuits between them on the table, she filled their bowls to the brim with the buttery potato soup and they sat down together.

Sipping the steaming soup, Billy said, "Mum, Rock's family has moved away and I think Sammy wants to pal around with me again. He didn't say so, but I could tell. Trouble is, him and Hawk don't like each other. I don't know what to do."

His mother crumpled a soda biscuit thoughtfully.

"Which one do you want for your friend, Bingo?"

"Both, I guess."

"Well, wasn't Sammy your friend first?"

"Yeah, but . . . "

"And didn't you tell me you only made friends with Danny because you were afraid of him? Maybe you figured he'd make a better friend than an enemy . . . "

Billy tipped the bowl and finished his soup. Mum must be a mind-reader, he thought to himself.

"Maybe at first," he admitted. " 'Cause I'm not a good fighter and Hawk stuck up for me. But now I really like him. And I like his family, too, most of them, anyway. They're . . . they're . . . " He was at a loss for words.

"Well, they're different. I'll say that for them," his mother laughed.

"Yeah, and special, too."

"Everybody's special, Bingo."

"I'm not, Mum. I'm no good at anything." He rubbed his hand, which was still stinging from Buster's zinger.

"Oh, Billy-Bo-Bingo." His mother reached out and pinched his cheek as if he were a little kid. "You're good at lots of things. Mr. Vierkoetter says you're his best swimmer. And Mr. Little told me on parents' night that you're his top student. Why, I do declare, I think you're my smartest youngster. Even smarter than your sister Willa, and she was a gold medallist, you know."

He knew. Everybody knew. His parents never let anybody forget that Willa had won the gold medal for highest honours in her entrance class.

"But smart's not what I mean, Mum. I'd rather be strong, like Hawk. I'll bet there's nobody in the world who could beat Hawk in a fight."

"Joe Louis could," Mrs. Thomson said with a smile.

Hooting with laughter, Billy pushed back his chair, leaned over to give his mother a peck on the check, threw on his windbreaker and dashed out the door.

Chapter 13

Playing Hooky

Billy decided to do something about his problem the very next day, but when he knocked lightly on the Watsons' door on his way to school, Mrs. Watson opened it a crack and said, "Sammy's got the measles, Billy. We're under quarantine."

Then she quickly shut the door. Sure enough, there was a red MEASLES sign in the front window.

Billy saw Danny coming down the street, so he waited. It was a nice spring day in March and purple crocuses were poking their heads up through the melting snow.

Taking a big, deep breath, Billy said, "I smell spring!"

Danny didn't answer. He seemed to be down in the dumps.

"What's the matter, Hawk?" Billy asked.

"I think I got spring fever," Danny said glumly.

"Me too," agreed Billy as he sniffed the air again.

"Geez, I'm sick of school," complained Danny, kicking a soggy snowbank. "And I need a rest from The Owl. I think the old geezer is starting to like me."

He stopped suddenly and grabbed Billy by the sleeve.

"Hey, Stretch, what do you say we play hooky?"

"Okay, but . . . "

"But what?"

"My mum will be mad if she finds out."

"So what? My old lady will kill me, but I don't care."

"Okay," agreed Billy. Danny's adventurous spirit was as contagious as the measles. "Where'll we go so we don't get caught?"

"I dunno. We could go downtown to the show. *Dive Bomber* is on at the Imperial. And we could stop at your Aunt's store and get some nuts."

"No we couldn't. Aunt Susan would tell on me."

"Well, then, let's go hunting or fishing," suggested Danny. "You got a gun, Stretch?"

"Nope. My Aunt Aggie in Muskoka, she's got two guns: a .22 and a 30-30. And Arthur's got a BB gun, but my mum hid it when he went off to the war."

"Okay, so let's go fishing. I got a couple of rods under my bed."

"Where'll we get worms?"

"I'll make worms, you'll see."

Sneaking through back alleys, they made their way to Danny's place.

"Where'll we go fishing, Hawk? The lake's too rough. I read in last night's paper that two men were swept off the pier at the mouth of the Humber and their bodies haven't been washed up yet."

"So we'll go to the pond. It's still froze solid."

"Are you sure?"

"Sure I'm sure. It takes more than one thaw to melt the Grenadier. The ice is three feet thick."

Turning into the lane behind the Cut-Rate, they saw the Chinese laundryman, his mouth full of clothespegs as usual. He glared at them balefully over the long underwear he was pegging.

"Will he tell?" whispered Billy.

"Nah. He don't even speak English," answered Danny.

Stealthily they crept up the back stairs into the big kitchen. It was empty except for Angel.

"Beat it!" squawked the noisy bird.

"Shut your yap, Angel!" hissed Danny, throwing the cover over the cage. Then he went to the refrigerator, took out a plate of bologna that was curled at the edges, laid the slices on a breadboard and cut them into thin strips that looked like real worms.

"Help yourself, Stretch," he said, and they both filled their pockets with the homemade worms.

Then Danny got the fishing rods from under his

bed and a small hatchet from his dad's toolbox.

"Okay, we're all set," he said. "Let's go."

Weaving their way through back alleys and up and down the hilly ravine called the Camel's Back, they came out onto Ellis Avenue.

And there, across the road, lay the wide, white Grenadier. Glistening ice covered the pond and sparkled like crushed diamonds in the sun.

The two boys dashed across the road and made their way out onto the ice. Swinging the hatchet, Danny led the way.

"We'll chop a hole in the middle. That's where the fish are," he said.

Billy followed in his footsteps, toting his fishing rod over his shoulder. As they trudged towards the middle of the lake, Billy noticed that some of the ice was beginning to get slushy, and he thought he felt a strange swaying sensation under his feet.

He stopped suddenly.

"It's moving, Hawk!" he cried, a wave of panic washing over him.

Billy saw fear flit briefly across Danny's face, then instantly disappear.

"That ain't nothing but currents under the ice. This here pond is bottomless."

"Yeah, I know."

Like every Swansea-born-and-bred kid, Billy knew by heart the stories about the mysterious Grenadier. It was said that one winter many years ago, a whole regiment of Grenadier Guards had crashed through the ice and drowned. And that's how the pond got its name. Suddenly he pictured as plain as day the slimy green bones of the soldiers and their horses all mingled together down in the bottomless deep. Cold shivers ran up his spine.

"This here looks like a good spot."

Stopping a few feet ahead of Billy, Danny dropped his rod and began hacking through the ice.

At that very moment, a cracking noise like the sound of breaking glass splintered the air and Billy felt the ice vibrate beneath his feet. Looking down, he was horrified to see black water seeping through a jagged hole. He tried to run, but his feet began sinking and almost instantly his rubber boots filled with slush.

"Help! Hawk!" he screamed in terror as he felt himself being sucked under.

Danny's head snapped back and his eyes widened with horror.

"Don't move, Stretch! Don't struggle!" he yelled.

Then he hastily wrapped the strong fishing line around his waist, threw himself flat out on the shifting ice and flung the end of his fishing rod toward his friend.

Billy grabbed hold with all his might, but his icy mitts immediately slipped off his hands and he felt himself sinking further and further into the icy water.

"Hawk, save me!" he screamed.

"Grab ahold again!" ordered Danny grimly.

With his bare hands, Billy grabbed the rod and hung on for dear life.

His shoulders hunched, his muscles straining, his head bent so low that his black hair splayed out like a mat on the ice, Danny began to pull.

Inching his way backward, he hauled with all his strength, and little by little Billy emerged from the gaping hole. By the time his legs appeared, his boots and socks had been sucked right off his feet.

Danny didn't waste a second. He unceremoniously hoisted Billy to his feet, and, giving the gaping hole a wide berth, he half-carried, half-dragged his friend back across the ice to the safety of the bank where they both collapsed in a soaking mass.

"I ain't as strong as I used to be," Danny gasped, his chest heaving.

"I'm freezing, Hawk!" cried Billy, shivering uncontrollably.

Danny took a deep breath and got on his hands and knees. "Climb on my back," he ordered.

Crying in misery, Billy just managed to crawl onto Danny's back.

Danny carried him home.

* * *

"Oh, the Lord have mercy!" Fran Thomson cried as Danny Thunder came stumbling through the kitchen door with Billy plastered to his back. They landed in a tangled, soggy heap on the shiny linoleum.

Grabbing the towel from the rack above the sink, Fran dropped to her knees and stripped off her son's sopping breeches. Then she began rubbing his blue legs vigorously. The day was a mild one, so his goose-flesh skin soon changed from blue to red.

Breathlessly, Mrs. Thomson rose to her feet.

"Now get yourself upstairs into dry clothes," she ordered through tight lips, "and bring the wet ones down."

Billy limped away in his soggy underwear and Danny turned towards the kitchen door.

"Stop where you are, young man!" snapped Fran. "You're not going anywhere until I get to the bottom of this affair. You sit yourself down right there."

Danny sat on the chair by the stove that Mrs. Thomson pointed to. He had never seen her angry before. He watched her nervously as she began furiously mopping up the muddy puddle.

Slowly the heat from the stove seeped through Danny's wet clothes and a cloud of steam began to rise around him.

Billy came back down, still shivering, and threw the wet clothes down the cellar stairs. He was afraid to look at his mother.

"Sit!" commanded his mother.

He sat at the kitchen table, his eyes glued to the floor.

"Now, out with it!" she snapped.

Through chattering teeth Billy told her everything. Hawk sat perfectly still, his head down, his long black lashes hiding his eyes.

When Billy was finished, his mother didn't speak. Instead she just shook her head in dismay, put the kettle on to boil and fetched three mugs down from the kitchen cabinet. Not a word was spoken until they were all sitting around the table, warming their hands on hot cocoa.

Then, in a conspiratorial whisper, she said to Danny, "Because you saved my boy's life, and because I'm thankful to the Almighty that you're both safe, we'll keep what happened today a dark secret between us. We won't breathe a word to a living soul."

"Especially Dad," Billy sighed in relief.

"Not a living, breathing soul," repeated his mother. "But only if you both swear by all that's good and holy that you'll never do such a wicked thing again as long as you live."

Now Danny raised his head and met her troubled eyes.

"I'm sorry, Mrs. Thomson," he said. "It was all my fault. Stretch wouldn't have thought of it hisself."

"I'm sorry, too, Mum," Billy said.

With a little cry she jumped up and threw her arms around them both. Then she stroked the lank black hair back from Danny's forehead.

"You're a real hero, Danny-boy," she said with a

catch in her voice. "And it's a shame your bravery will have to go unrecognized. You could've just run for help, but if you had done that, my Bingo would be at the bottom of that pond this very minute."

Shaking her head again, she put the mugs in the dishpan in the sink.

"You remind me of my father," she continued, turning the tap on. "Puppa saved many a drowning soul from the Grenadier, and never a bit of credit would he take. He was an unsung hero, Puppa was, and so are you, Danny-boy."

She looked at the clock on the wall. "School will be out soon. You'd better run straight home, Danny, and get out of those wet clothes."

"Who'll write your hooky note, Hawk?" Billy asked.

"I'll write my own. I can write exactly like my ma."

"For mercy sakes, I don't want to hear another word," cried Fran Thomson, clapping her hands over her ears. "Away you go, now, Danny, and do whatever you have to do, but don't tell me about it."

* * *

That night at the supper table, Billy couldn't stop shivering. His mother felt his forehead and remarked that he must be catching something. Then she sent him to bed with a hot water bottle.

As he lay alone in the bed, his mother's words

kept repeating in his mind like a broken record.

"You're a real hero, Danny-boy!" she had gushed. "Danny-boy," for pete's sake. She had even compared him to her own father, and everybody in Swansea knew that Grampa Cole was a hero. Bea was forever going on about him.

For the first time since their friendship had begun, Billy felt really jealous of Hawk. He felt like the hundred-pound weakling in the comic pages who was always having to be rescued by strongman Charles Atlas. He hated having to be rescued all the time. It was like having a bodyguard. And he didn't want Hawk for a bodyguard. He wanted him for a friend.

"He deserves a medal," his mother had said after Danny left. Then she had actually smiled — smiled when her own son had darn near drowned, for corn sake!

Boy, if she only knew some of the stuff he does, Billy thought. Like throwing mudballs all over the Chinaman's clean bedclothes. And snatching apples and bananas off the fruitman's cart. And once he even stole a quarter out of his own mother's purse. Billy recounted more and more of Danny's faults and misdemeanours to himself. And the more faults he recounted, the better he felt.

He rolled over onto his side, drew the hot water bottle up between his long feet and hugged his knees to his bony chest.

"Some hero, picking on a poor little man who can't

even speak English," Billy grumbled in the midst of a long yawn.

At last he stopped thinking and let his eyes drop shut as he fell into an exhausted sleep.

He dreamed he was the pilot of a bomber and Danny was one of the gunners. They were attacked and shot down by a German Messerschmitt and they both had to bail out. But Danny's chute didn't open and Billy saved his life by grabbing him in midair.

Chapter 14

Sick of the Bell

In the middle of the night, Billy woke the whole house with a barking cough.

His mother rose wearily, came in and felt his forehead and went downstairs to make a mustard plaster. While he waited, he got up to go to the bathroom. Then he came back to bed and sneezed all over Jakey.

"You stoopid jerk!" yelled Jakey, vaulting out of bed. Scrubbing his face on his pyjama sleeve, he grabbed his pillow and headed for the stairs. His mother was hurrying up the staircase with the reeking plaster.

"Where are you off to, Jakey?" she whispered when she saw him.

"I'm gonna sleep on the chesterfield before Billy

drowns me in his germs," he grumbled.

"That's a good idea. I'll throw you down a quilt."

The fumes from the mustard plaster knocked Billy right out, and the next day he woke up feeling much better.

"I'm going to keep you home from school today just to be on the safe side," his mother said. Then she added with a sigh of relief, "At least I won't have to tell a lie in a note to the teacher. Now you just stay in bed, and when I've got a minute I'll bring you a nice poached egg on toast."

She fluffed up his pillow and then, with one quick swipe, ripped the plaster off his chest.

"Ouch!" Billy yelped, looking down his nose at the bright red patch spreading across his skinny rib cage.

"Believe me, it hurts a lot less if I pull it off quickly like that," his mother assured him. "Now you cover up, then after you're fortified, maybe you'll feel like writing to Arthur. You haven't sent him a line since Christmas. He's your own brother, far from home."

As she descended the stairs, he heard her singing in a reproachful tone, "My Bonnie lies over the ocean . . ."

With the lovely taste of poached egg on buttery toast still lingering in his mouth, Billy propped himself up on two pillows and turned the tray upside down for a desk. He opened the lined writing tablet his mother had brought him and licked the end of the pencil she had sharpened with the butcher knife.

"March 19, 1944. A.D." he wrote.

Dear Arthur,

I'm home sick in bed, so Mum says I have to write to you. Did you get my last letter? If so why didn't you answer it? Do you think the war will last much longer? I hope so, because I'm going to join the air force when I am sixteen. I'm really tall for my age, so when I'm sixteen, I should be able to pass for eighteen. Jakey won't pass because he's too short. So ha! Ha!

I'll be twelve in November and Bea will be twenty-two. Wow, is she ever old!

Mum just came up to give me some Friar's Balsam on a teaspoon of sugar. She says to ask how you are.

Everyone is fine here, except Mum has wind around her heart and Jakey has a gumboil and Dad has lumbago again and I've got this here bad cold.

Oh, yeah, and guess what else?

Give up?

Okay, I'll tell you.

Our Willa is in the family way. Mum didn't tell me herself because she thinks I'm too young to hear that kind of stuff, but I heard her telling Mrs. Hubbard (Ada-May's mother; have you still got a crush on Ada-May?) over the back fence.

That means we're going to be uncles and I'm

only eleven-and-a-half years old, for pete's sake.

Bea's okay, but she's changed a lot. Remember I used to be her favourite because I was born on her birthday and she didn't get any other present? Well, ever since she married that stupid Lorne Huntley, he's all she ever thinks about. When she shows his picture in his Air Force uniform, all her girlfriends go gaga and swear he looks like Gary Cooper because of his dimples. Do you think Lorne looks like Gary Cooper? I don't. Anyway, because he's so handsome, she's always worried that some English girl might entice him away.

We've heard some lurid rumours about those English girls being terrible flirts. Do you know anything about that, Arthur? I thought maybe if you wrote to Bea and told her they were all ugly dumb-Doras she wouldn't worry so much. Anyway it might be worth a try.

2:30 p.m. Same day.

Gosh, I fell asleep without knowing it and just woke up. Mum says that proves how sick I am. She rubbed me with camphorated oil. It stinks like anything, but it feels nicer than the mustard plaster that she gave me last night.

Well . . . let me see, what else can I tell you?

Oh, yeah. I have a new friend that I don't think you know about. His name is Danny Thunder (short for Thundercloud). I call him

Hawk because he's one-quarter Mohawk Indian. He looks like an Indian, too. He's got straight black hair that nearly touches his shoulders, high cheekbones, brown skin and black eyes.

Bea says he's going to be a lady-killer when he grows up. He thinks she's gorgeous, even if she is old.

Hawk's nickname for me is Stretch because I'm so much taller than he is. But he's a lot stronger than me, and that makes me mad. I'm five feet nine inches in my bare feet. Mum says if I keep it up, I'll be taller than her father, who was six feet tall when he was alive. How tall are you, Arthur?

I guess the war is way worse in England because we don't get bombed over here. But Mum had to make blackout curtains to cover the windows just in case.

You know Mr. Mortimer from up the street (the one who doesn't have to go to war because he has twelve kids), well he's our air-raid warden. He thinks he's a big shot because he gets to wear a white helmet and a white armband with C.D.C. on it. Dad says he ought to try wearing a real uniform.

Anyway, he came to inspect our blackout curtains because he said he could see light at the bottom of our front window. Then he nailed a big

A.R.P. instruction card inside our front door. It tells us to go down into the cellar in case of an air raid.

The minute he left, Mum ripped the sign down and stuck it in the buffet drawer. She said she wasn't having that unsightly thing on her front door.

Dad says it's just a bunch of hogwash anyway, because there'll never be an air raid here. That's why we sent you boys over there, to blast Hitler to smithereens. I think he's right, for once.

We have other war problems too. For instance, some of our food is rationed. And we have to buy war savings stamps at school out of our own money. My stamp book is nearly full. There are pictures of Hitler and Mussolini and Tojo in the book and you stamp out their ugly faces.

Oh, yeah, and guess what happened to Aunt Myrtle? She got caught hoarding. The law says only three-quarters of a pound of sugar per person, but Aunt Myrtle had an extra pound stashed away in her cupboard and somebody snitched (nobody knows who) and she got fined five dollars.

Aunt Ellie says she thinks she knows who the snitcher is, but she's not telling because she doesn't want any busybodies poking their noses into her sugar bowl!

Arthur with Mum.

Mum's a bit worried, too, about Hawk's mother, Mrs. Thunder. She's really swell and calls me Peaches because of my peach-fuzz moustache. I think I'll need to shave soon. Jakey shaves once a week already.

Anyway, Mrs. Thunder works at the Cut-Rate Meat Market in the cashier's booth and gives us meat without taking the coupons out of our book. Mum's worried she'll be caught red-handed like Aunt Myrtle. But Mrs. Thunder says not to worry, she knows what she's doing. She does too. She knows all kinds of tricks. Mum says she's a good scout.

The weather here is warming up. We got our last coal delivery yesterday. Mum had just brought up my poached egg on toast when she heard the first bagful go rattling down the chute. So she ran down the stairs to the cellar to count the bags because Aunt Ellie says the coal man is a cheater.

She says he cheated her out of one whole bag, but she couldn't prove it. Now she makes him wait while she counts all the empty bags.

Speaking of the coal man reminds me that tonight is Tuesday, which means my favourite program is on the radio.

Blue Coal presents . . . The Shadow Knows . . . Ha! Ha! Ha!

Last week the announcer said in his creepiest

voice that tonight's story is called "Death Stalks the Shadow." I'll bet you don't hear such swell stories on the wireless, eh, Arthur? Jakey says that's what they call the radio in Pongoland. (That's what Jakey calls England. I don't know why.)

All of a sudden I've got a headache. So . . . to be continued.

March 20, 1944, A.D.

Hi Arthur!

I slept right through supper time yesterday and I still had my headache, so Mum gave me a big dose of Epsom salts to flush me out. Ugh, I thought I was poisoned! Mum said it would either kill me or cure me. Well, I had the runs all night, but I feel better today. So she was right, as usual.

Oh, yeah. I forgot to tell you that gasoline is also rationed, but we don't care because we haven't got a car. Dad doesn't even know how to drive, for corn sake.

When I'm sixteen, I'm going to make a pile of money and buy a Hudson car like Cousin Harry's.

Do you still get seasick, Arthur? Or are you used to it by now? I get seasick. That's why I want to be an airman instead of a sailor. Last summer, when Sammy Watson and me went on a ferryboat ride to Niagara-on-the-Lake, we both spent the whole trip throwing up in the can.

Now that spring is here (tomorrow is the first day), Hawk and I are going to build a clubhouse in our backyard at the end of Mum's victory garden. Mum said we could because Hawk doesn't have a backyard. You see, the Thunders live in the flat above the Cut-Rate and the back stairs lead right into the alleyway.

I hope Hawk will let Sammy join our club too. Hawk and Sammy don't hit it off, but Mum says Hawk should let Sammy join because the more the merrier. I like them both and don't know what to do about it.

Did I tell you I got a bike for Christmas? Mum says not to tell you. She says you might be jealous because you never had a bike when you were my age because of the Depression. It's not a new one, it's used. And anyway, it's not my fault that you never had a bike. It's a swell black Victory bike. Right now it's leaning beside the coal bin because Mum won't let me take it out until all the snow's gone.

If my cold is better by Saturday, Jakey says he'll take me to a wrestling match at Maple Leaf Gardens. Somebody on his paper route gave him two free tickets. Whipper Billy Watson is fighting Nanjo Singh. Jakey says the Whip will beat Singh all holler because he's the champion *of the world. I said, 'Maybe the fights are fixed,' and Jakey punched me and said, 'How's that for fixed?'*

What kind of toothpaste do they give you in the navy, Arthur? Mum bought us Ipana for a change from baking soda. It's supposed to whiten your teeth in no time, but I've been using it for a week and mine aren't getting any whiter. Dad says it's all hogwash, you can't beat salt and water.

Anyway, I only wish I could tell you how I got this awful cold, because it would be a lot more interesting than all this malarkey, but Mum swore Hawk and me to secrecy. Maybe by the time the war is over and you come home it'll be okay to tell you.

Bea said she's going to stop off at Aunt Susan's store tonight on the way home from work to get candies and nuts to make Lorne a love box. (Those are Bea's words, not mine!) Aunt Susan always gives the best mixture (giant cashews, Brazil nuts and pecans, no peanuts) for you servicemen. She says it's her contribution to the war effort. She only sends us the cheap mixture, mostly peanuts. But I don't mind because I like peanuts, especially redskins.

Mum says I got to rest now, so . . . to be continued.

March 21, 1944, A.D.
11:00 a.m. E.S.T.
Guess what? Aunt Susan sent us the best mixture too.

I said, "Oh, boy, pecans!" and Bea said, "They're not pee-cans, they're pek-awns. A pee-can is something you use when you're lost in the bush and can't find a toilet." I nearly died laughing, but Mum told Bea not to be rude.

Well, I guess that's all for now. I never intended to write so much stuff, but there's nothing else to do here in bed.

Mum wants me to study for my Easter exams, but I don't need to because I already know everything. Grade seven is easy as pie. I'll be glad to get into grade eight. Another reason I'll be glad is I'll be rid of The Owl.

Miss Nattress is the grade eight teacher and she's a real good looker.

Mum just came up with some hot lemonade and she saw all these pages spread all over the bed. She says it'll cost a fortune to mail, but I said if I don't get a personal reply it'll be my last letter anyway.

So . . .

Deliver de letter, de sooner de better,
De later de letter, de madder I getter.
From your young bro. Bill.
P.S. I'm collecting war posters. Can you

*send me some? I have pictures of Spitfires and
Hurricanes and destroyers and cruisers and
tanks tacked all over our bedroom walls. Jakey
says the room looks like a war zone. I thought
Mum would make me take them down, but she
didn't. W.R.T.*

* * *

A few days later, Billy felt a lot better and his mother
decided to send him to school. While he ate his Cream
of Wheat with a well of liquid honey in the middle,
Fran sat at the end of the table frowning over what
was left of the writing tablet.

"I wonder what I should put in the note to your
teacher?" she puzzled.

Then her brown eyes began to twinkle and she
chuckled almost mischievously. As she dipped the
pen into the ink bottle, she said, "I think I'll just say
that Billy-Bo-Bingo was absent from school for four
days because he was sick of the bell."

"For pete's sake, Mum, don't say that. The Owl's
got no sense of humour. It'll only make him mad."

"Oh, pshaw, what a pity. My mother made up that
joke," she said.

Then she wrote a careful note to impress the
teacher.

Mrs. Thomson handed Billy the note. Then she
looked at him gravely and said, "Now you remember

your promise to steer clear of the pond, or I'll have to tell your father what happened and he'll skin you alive with the razor strop."

"I will, Mum. Don't worry. I've never been so scared in my life."

Billy finished his porridge, stuffed the note into the back pocket of his breeches and put on his outdoor clothes.

With his hand on the doorknob he said, "Mum, if Hawk calls for me today, will you tell him I left early?"

"Yas. But why are you leaving so early? The school's only a hop, skip and jump away."

"I'm going to call for Sammy, but don't tell Hawk that, okay?"

"All right. But I won't lie for you, Billy. I'll just say that you've left. Now pull your earflaps down and wrap your muffler around your mouth. I don't want you to catch your death of pneumonia."

"Thanks, Mum." Billy ran out the door, his earflaps flapping, his muffler flying in the wind.

Chapter 15

Capitulation

Billy knocked softly on the door under the War Worker Sleeping sign.

Sammy opened it.

"What do you want?" he hissed.

"Let's be pals again," Billy answered simply.

Sammy frowned and snorted and looked at his feet, but he didn't shut the door.

"What'll Hawk say?" he asked.

The question made Billy bristle.

"Hawk doesn't own me," he snapped.

"Yeah, but . . . "

Just then Mrs. Watson appeared in the doorway behind Sammy. Turning him around, she did up the top button of his windbreaker.

"There's no friends like old friends," she said.

Then she winked at Billy over her son's leather helmet and shoved Sammy unceremoniously out the door.

Sammy had his baseball with him, so as soon as they got to the schoolyard they started playing catch.

When Danny arrived, he spotted them right away and marched towards them with an angry look on his face.

Billy's heart skipped a beat, but he forced a friendly grin on his face and cried, "Hi, Hawk! Here, catch," and threw the ball.

Danny sidestepped and the ball fell unheeded to the ground. Then he walked right up to Billy, fixed him with a steely gaze, jabbed his thumb in Sammy's direction and growled, "Make up your mind, Stretch. It's either him or me."

Billy felt gooseflesh creeping all over his body, but he knew it was now or never. He had to stand up to Danny.

Forcing himself to look Danny straight in the eye, he said, "How come I have to pick? Why can't we all be friends?" His voice wavered and cracked, but at least he had spoken his mind.

Danny could hardly believe his ears. Punching his right fist into his cupped left hand he snarled, " 'Cause I say so, that's why."

Dead silence followed.

Then Danny said, "Ah, who needs ya, anyway."

Jamming his fists in his pockets, he hunched his shoulders, turned on his heel with a crunch of gravel and angrily strode away.

After that, Danny turned his back and walked away whenever Billy tried to talk to him.

* * *

One night after supper, Bea was sitting by the radio listening to Glenn Miller's Band playing "Don't Sit Under the Apple Tree with Anyone Else But Me" while mending a ladder in her stocking when she said, "I miss seeing Danny Thunder around here. What's happened between you two?"

Billy felt the sting of jealousy again, but he had to admit to himself that he missed Danny, too. "Aw, he's sore because me and Sammy are pals again," he explained. "I like Sammy okay, but I like Hawk better. Sammy's boring compared to Hawk."

"You can say that again," laughed Bea as she rolled her stockings in a ball. Then she remarked, to no one in particular, "I'll be glad when the weather warms up so I can wear Leg Do instead of stockings. You can't buy a decent pair of silk hose for love nor money since the war started."

"Well, I don't like that Leg Do paint," her mother said, looking up from the regulation navy socks she was knitting Arthur. "It rubs off on the bedclothes and makes a terrible mess."

Bea promptly changed the subject. "Why can't the three of you be friends, Billy?" she asked.

" 'Cause Hawk says it's either him or Sammy. I have to pick."

"Well, that's a shame," his mother put in. "I thought he was a nicer boy than that. Oh, drat!" she cried as she tried to catch some dropped stitches.

"I miss Hawk's old lady too," Billy continued now that he'd got their attention again.

"William Robert Thomson!" His mother threw up her hands and dropped more stitches. "Don't you dare call Violet Thunder an old lady. What do you think that makes me? And just see what you made me do!" She poked her fingers through the hole in her knitting.

"Heck, Mum, I don't mean it that way. All the Thunder kids call their mother that, so it just comes natural. And they call their father their old man, too. But they really like their parents, even if they are sort of . . . " He shrugged, trying to find the right words to describe Mr. and Mrs. Thunder.

"Unconventional?" suggested Bea.

"Yeah, are they ever." Billy started to snicker. "Do you know what Mr. Thunder says when he breaks wind, Mum?"

"No. But I'll wager you're about to tell me."

"Well, when he lets go a real ripper, he guffaws his head off and blames the dog."

"I didn't know they had a dog."

Billy laughed so hard he had trouble getting out the punch line. "That's exactly what Mrs. Thunder always says, 'Elwood, you flaming idiot, we haven't got a dog!' "

Bea yelped with laughter and her mother threw Arthur's unfinished sock into the air and wiped her eyes on her apron.

Mrs. Thomson got up and put the kettle on to boil. When it was whistling merrily, she made tea for Bea and herself and a cup of cocoa for Billy.

After they had finished their tea, they went into the dining room to pack ditty bags for Lorne and Arthur. An assortment of goods was spread out on the table: two bars of Lifebuoy health soap, two wooden bowls of shaving cream, razor blades, Spearmint gum, Jenny Lind chocolates and two boxes of Aunt Susan's best nut mixtures.

Lovingly they began preparing the packages while Billy watched enviously.

It must be swell to get a ditty bag, he thought.

"Oh, pshaw, I'd hoped to have the socks ready to go," Fran said as she added a tin of home baking to each bag.

"Never mind, Mum," Bea said. "You can put them in next week."

When the ditty bags, which weren't bags at all but corrugated cardboard boxes, were securely tied and addressed, Billy brought up his problem again.

"Bea, what do you think I should do about Hawk and Sammy? Did you and Glad and Ruthie ever fight when you were young?"

Bea rolled her eyes at the reference to her age and replied, "Sure we did. But we always talked it out and patched things up. That's why we're still a threesome."

"Yeah, but the trouble is, Hawk won't even talk to me. His mother says he's stubborn as a mule."

Jakey passed by on his way upstairs. "Why don't you tell the jerk to go fly a kite!" was his advice.

"You drop dead!" Billy snapped.

He started pacing back and forth, muttering to himself, until Bea finally yelled at him in exasperation, "For pity sakes, Billy, stop it. I'm trying to write a letter and I can't hear myself think."

The outburst made Mr. Thomson look up from reading the evening news and put in his two cents worth.

"Settle down and get at your homework," he barked. "You're not so smart you don't need to study."

Billy opened his books beside Bea on the dining room table and pretended to study.

* * *

The next day when he came home from school, Billy's mother said, "There's something I want you to do for me, Bingo."

"Can't it wait, Mum? I have to do my paper route. If I'm late, Mr. Mortimer gets mad and says he won't pay me."

"No, it can't wait. You tell that old skinflint you had to do a job for your mother."

Hopping up on the little stool, Fran got her purse down and took out a two-dollar bill.

"Now you hightail it up to the Cut-Rate Meat Market as fast as your legs will carry you and get me a nice ham bone. I want to make split-pea soup for supper." She pressed the wrinkled yellow two-dollar bill into his hand. "And don't lose the change. That's my last cent until your father gets his pay packet on Saturday."

Billy stuffed the money into his pocket and went back out the door. When he got to Bloor Street, he looked furtively up and down, hoping he would not see Hawk or any of his brothers. The coast was clear, so he sidled into the Cut-Rate behind another customer. Quickly he asked Mr. Weiner for a large ham bone and then lined up to pay at the wicket.

When Violet Thunder saw Billy, her bright red lipstick broke into a beaming smile.

"Peaches!" she cried in a raucous voice that turned every head in the store. "What hole have you been hiding in? I've missed them baby blue peepers."

Billy blushed and answered, "I've missed you, too, Mrs. Thunder. How's Mr. Thunder?"

"Oh, he's large as life and twice as ugly. He keeps asking Danny, 'Where's Skinny?' but that ornery young whelp won't tell us a thing. Is anything wrong between you, Peaches? Did that boy of mine beat you up or somethin'? If he did, he'll be sorry, I can tell you!"

There it was again, the notion that Danny was the invincible man and that he, Billy, was the weakling that always needed protection.

"Heck, no, Mrs. Thunder. It's nothing like that . . . but . . . but . . . "

"But what?" She motioned him to come to the side door of the wicket.

The customers lined up behind Billy began to grumble and shuffle their feet in the sawdust.

"Just hold your horses!" Violet Thunder bellowed at them, then she whispered to Billy, "Now out with it!"

"Well, Hawk is sore at me because I made up with Sammy Watson. You see, Mrs. Thunder, me and Sammy were best buddies before Hawk came to our school, and, well, I dropped him like a hot potato for Hawk. Now I want us all to be friends. You know, like the Three Musketeers. But Hawk says I have to choose. It's either him or Sammy. And I can't drop Sammy again. It wouldn't be fair. Besides, Hawk won't even talk to me, so I don't know what to do."

Mrs. Thunder knitted her pencilled brows and pursed her painted lips. Suddenly her face lit up like a light bulb.

"You know what, Peaches? I've got a hunch that young varmint feels as bad as you do. That's why he's upstairs right now sulking like a two-year-old. So why don't you just go on up there and give him a piece of your mind?"

"Okay, Mrs. Thunder!" Billy was so glad of the advice that he almost forgot to pay for the ham bone. Quickly he paid, pocketed the change and headed up the dark staircase that led to the flat above the store.

A crack of light showed under the door. Billy tapped lightly. Seconds passed and there was no answer, so he doubled his fist and rapped hard with his knuckles. Still no answer.

He was just about to give up when Danny's voice yelled through the door, "Who's there?"

"It's me, Stretch Thomson. Can I come in, Hawk?"

Silence. Billy's heart flopped, then all of a sudden he got mad and was just about to pound on the door when it flew open.

There stood Hawk in his red flannel drawers, his black eyes flashing, his long hair straggly.

"Whadda you want?" he growled.

"Can I come in, Hawk? I need to talk to you."

"We got nothing to say to each other." Leaving the door wide open, Danny turned his back and strode away, towards his bedroom. With a long-legged leap like a giant frog, Billy jumped in front of Danny and blocked his way.

Caught off guard, Danny looked startled. Billy had never dared get in his way before.

"Move!" he demanded.

Billy placed his hands on his hips. "You'll have to

make me, Hawk," he said grimly.

Danny looked more perplexed than angry. He frowned, flexed his muscles, clenched and un-clenched his fists.

Billy's muscles were flexing too — his stomach muscles — but this time he was determined not to back down.

They glared at each other, eyeball to eyeball.

Suddenly, Danny snickered a little and blew through his nose as he tried to stifle a laugh. Billy nervously did the same, a smile twitching the corners of his mouth. Then Danny let go. He threw back his head and roared.

"Geez, Stretch! Are you trying to get yourself killed, or what?"

Hooting outright with laughter now, they lunged at each other and rolled on the floor in a mock wrestling match.

Then they talked their troubles out over a huge bottle of Kik Cola. By the time the pop was gone, they were pals again.

"Okay, okay," Danny finally agreed. "Watson can come with us once in a while. But not all the time. I hate the way he snorts his nose. Can't he talk without snorting?"

"I'll make him stop," Billy promised.

"And another thing." Danny's dark-winged eyebrows drew together menacingly. "I'm still the boss of this outfit. You got that, Stretch?"

"Got it! Anything you say, Hawk." Billy had decided to let Danny save face. "I gotta go now, Hawk. My mum's waiting for the ham bone and I'm late with my paper route. Old man Mortimer won't pay me if his paper's late."

"Aw, you leave that crackpot to me," Danny said. "I'll get your money for you."

Billy didn't answer, but he thought to himself, Oh, sure. Here we go again. Hawk to the rescue.

Chapter 16

Terrible War News

Billy's mother was pleased as punch with the ham bone because it was thick with meat and marrow. After he had given it to her, he hightailed it all over the neighbourhood delivering his papers.

When he got back home again, he handed his mother the leftover newspaper and ran breathlessly up to the bathroom. He was just about bursting from all that Kik Cola.

The moment he came back downstairs, his stomach easing with relief, he knew something was wrong. His mother was sitting by the stove, her face ashen white, the newspaper clutched to her breast.

"What's the matter, Mum?" he cried anxiously.

She just shook her head and held up the paper,

pointing with a trembling finger to the black, two-inch headlines:

NUREMBERG RAID, TRAGIC DISASTER.
BOMBER COMMAND SUFFERS
HEAVIEST LOSSES OF WAR.

The story continued: "Out of 779 bombers to take part in the raid, 96 have been reported missing."

The awful news made Billy's flesh crawl.

"Would Lorne be in that raid, Mum?" he whispered.

"I think so," she whispered back, and as she spoke they heard Bea's high heels clicking up the alleyway.

"Oh, mercy, hide the paper!" Mrs. Thomson cried.

Billy looked frantically for a hiding place. Grabbing the lifter, he removed the stove lid, stuffed the paper in, and clanked the lid back on just as Bea came in the door.

But it didn't do much good to hide the paper, because that sort of news could not be hidden for long. The memory of that awful day — March 30, 1944 — would live forever in history.

* * *

For two long weeks Bea went back and forth to work like a ghost, white with worry and fatigue.

And night after night she paced the hallway endlessly.

Then Billy would hear his mother get up and whisper, "Come downstairs, Booky, and I'll make you a nice cup of tea."

At long last came the blessed news. Lorne and the crew of the Lancaster had survived by nothing short of a miracle. But the letter was so heavily censored that Bea didn't find out what the miracle was until the war was over and her young husband was safely home.

"Our Lanky, which, as you know, is named Beatrice after guess who," wrote Lorne, "brought us safely back to dear old England. Boy, will I have stories to tell my grandchildren when I'm an old man in a rocking chair."

But the joy in Billy's house at the wonderful news was dampened by the pain in the home of his Aunt Martha, one of his mother's many sisters. Her oldest son, Garnett, who was a rear gunner and had just turned twenty-one, had been lost over the English Channel.

Months later, although Aunt Martha vowed she'd never give up hope, a memorial service was held and a special poem was read in Garnett's honour:

The pain is gone, for I am dead,
My time on earth is done,
But though a hundred years may pass,
I'll still be twenty-one.

Throughout the sad service Billy sat remembering the last time he'd seen his cousin. Garnett had been on embarkation leave and had come to say goodbye.

Mrs. Thomson had kissed his smooth cheek and had said she would pray for him. He had laughed and said he would be fine. Mr. Thomson had shaken his hand and had wished him Godspeed. Jakey had given him a punch and had called him a lucky son-of-a-gun. Bea had kissed him, unable to speak.

Then Garnett had said he had time to kill, would Billy like to go to the show, his treat?

They had seen *My Friend Flicka* at the Runnymede, and every time Roddy McDowell cried they had burst out laughing.

Tears rolled down Billy's face, remembering.

After that mournful day, the war did not seem so glamorous anymore. Billy often stayed out of the house because he couldn't bear to see his mother so worried and fearful all the time. Whenever there was a knock at the door, especially at night, her hand would fly to her throat, expecting bad news.

* * *

So, Billy spent more and more time at Danny's place, because Danny's family was untouched by the war.

"I don't know a living soul over there," Mrs. Thunder declared one time, and Mr. Thunder was

149

heard to remark that the war was in fact good for his business.

Every Saturday afternoon, Stretch and Hawk and Snort, which was Sammy's inevitable nickname, would hang around together.

It didn't take Sammy long to learn the rules. As long as he never crossed Hawk, and followed his lead in all things, and remembered not to snort his nose, he got along just fine with Danny Thunder.

As the days grew warmer and longer, the three boys began to go out together after supper as well, even on week nights.

One balmy May evening, Sammy was standing on the mat just inside the Thomsons' kitchen door while Mrs. Thomson gave Billy his orders.

"Now don't you be out late. It's a school night, you know. Have you done your homework?"

"No, Mum. I don't need to. I know all that grade seven bunk. I hope grade eight is harder, because I'm getting bored."

Just then he heard his dad's footsteps clumping up the cellar stairs, so he and Sammy hightailed it out the back door to avoid another lecture.

They waited for Hawk behind the Meat Market, as arranged. Then, the second they laid eyes on him, they knew something was wrong.

"What's up, Hawk?" Billy asked a bit nervously.

"Didn't you hear the news?" Danny growled.

Sammy, who had a cold, forgot himself and let out a loud wet snort.

"Oh, geez, I'm sorry," he apologized.

"What news?" asked Billy as they made their way along Bloor Street, Sammy bringing up the rear.

"My old lady heard on the radio that the stupid city council has passed a curfew that says kids under sixteen can't be out at night after nine o'clock."

Billy just shrugged at the news. He was hardly ever out past nine anyway.

Then Sammy piped up, "Oh, well, it don't apply to us because we live in Swansea."

"When you're on Bloor Street you're in Toronto, stoopid!" sneered Danny.

"Then we only got a couple of hours left," Sammy said.

Danny shot a scornful glance over his shoulder at Sammy. "Are you kidding? I ain't paying no attention to any dumb law that tells me when I can or can't be out. My old man says the law is a ass."

"Dickens said that," Sammy, corrected him.

"Are you calling my old man a liar?" snapped Danny.

"No, Hawk," Billy intervened. "He means Mr. Bumble, one of Charles Dickens' characters, said that."

"Oh well, my old man says any law that sends kids to war to get killed when they're eighteen, but won't let them go to the late show if they want to when they're fifteen, is assin-somethin'."

"Asinine, and he's right," Billy agreed. "Your old man's smart."

"Yeah." Danny seemed satisfied. "Anyway, let's go to the show. Who's got cash?"

Billy and Sammy dug into their pockets and came up with some loose change.

"Hand it over," Danny demanded, and they each gave him their money.

"It's not enough, Hawk," Billy said.

"Leave that to me," Danny said.

They waited for a streetcar to trundle by and then dashed across the road to the Esquire theatre.

"You two wait over there and make like we're not together," Danny ordered.

Billy and Sammy went to the far side of the wicket and looked at the pictures advertising the coming attractions.

"Next week: Shirley Temple and Clark Gable in *Kathleen*. See adorable Shirley with the king of the movies in her most grown-up role yet!"

"Ugh!" Billy grunted.

"I second that," snorted Sammy.

Danny came up behind them and said, "Okay, I got the tickets. Let's go." And hurried off in the wrong direction. Billy and Sammy had to run to catch up.

"Why are we going away from the show?" asked Sammy.

"Shut up, Snort," barked Danny.

Ducking into the doorway of a closed shop, Danny took a penknife from his pocket. Then, with practiced fingers he inserted the tip of the blade into the edge of one of the tickets, pried it gently apart, and divided it in two.

"Presto!" he grinned, and gave Billy and Sammy the severed ticket.

"What if we get caught?" whispered Sammy.

"Don't!" warned Danny. "Now we'll separate and mix with the crowd. It'll work, you'll see. Me and my brothers do it all the time and we ain't never been caught yet."

So they jostled in amongst the moviegoers, handed their tickets to the doorman and bolted down the aisle.

"What did I tell ya," boasted Danny, slumping down and putting his feet up on the back of the seat in front of him. Billy laughed and Sammy snorted.

The show was great, a terrific gangster movie starring Edward G. Robinson and a newsreel that was two weeks old.

When they came out onto the street, it was pitch dark.

"I wonder what time it is?" Billy said.

"It feels awful late," ventured Sammy.

"I'm starved," declared Danny. "Let's go get some grub."

"We've got no money left," Sammy whined. "I'm

scared of the curfew," he whispered to Billy. "Let's go home now."

"Shut up and follow me," commanded their intrepid leader. Billy and Sammy obediently fell into step behind him.

As they neared Amodeo's Fruit Market, they saw Mr. Amodeo lugging a bushel basket of potatoes from the sidewalk display into the store.

"Perfect timing!" gloated Danny. "Ready! Set! Go!"

With Hawk in the lead, they streaked past the fruit stand and each grabbed an apple on the run.

At that very moment, Mrs. Amodeo stepped outside to help her husband.

"Help! Robbers! Police!" she shrieked.

As if on cue, a policeman appeared from a shop doorway where he had been checking the lock.

The boys saw him at the last minute. "Ditch the apples!" yelled Hawk, and he threw the one he was holding against the side of a passing streetcar, where it landed with a juicy splat. Billy and Sammy let their apples fall into the gutter.

The three boys continued running, but in their panic they forgot to change direction and all the policeman had to do was hold out his nightstick at knee level. Danny went down like a falling tree and Billy and Sammy sprawled on top of him.

"On yer feet, ye thieving varmints!" commanded the officer.

Then he marched them in front of him, prodding them with his stick, right into the Bloor Street police station.

Inside the station the officer ordered the three boys to sit on a bench by the wall while he conferred with the man in charge at the desk.

Sammy began crying quietly and Billy's face turned the colour of pie dough.

Danny stared straight ahead, expressionless, but out of the corner of his mouth he whispered, "I got us into this and I'll get us out. Keep your trap shut, Snort, if ya know what's good for ya."

The arresting policeman beckoned them up to the desk. Once again Danny took the lead.

Bold as brass, he marched right up to the sergeant's desk and said, "I got a right to a phone call."

Oh no, Billy thought, we'll end up in the slammer for sure now. But even as such black thoughts crossed his mind, he found himself grudgingly admiring Hawk's nerve.

The sergeant looked at Danny as though he was having the exact same thoughts as Billy. Without a word he plonked the cradle telephone with a loud jangle under Danny's nose.

Danny dialled a number, cupped his hand around the mouthpiece and turned his head away. He spoke in such a low whisper that all Billy could hear was the pounding of his own heart.

Danny plonked the telephone with an equally

loud jangle back in the middle of the wide wooden desk after his call and the boys were ordered back to the bench. The sergeant leaned down to listen to the rest of the constable's report.

Suddenly the doors to the police station flew open and in blew Elwood Thunder.

Both policemen snapped to attention.

Giving the three boys a baleful black stare, Elwood Thunder strode up to the desk and engaged in a hushed conversation with the two officers.

At the end of the discourse, the sergeant leaned back, clasped his hands behind his head, and laughed out loud.

"Ah, well now, Mr. Thunder," boomed the sergeant, "boys will be boys, you know. So we'll overlook their bit of jiggery-pokery this time and I'll release them into your capable hands."

When Elwood Thunder got the three culprits out onto the sidewalk, he cuffed his own son's ears and jabbed a finger in Billy's face.

"You get away home, Skinny," he ordered in the meanest voice Billy had ever heard him use, "and take your snotty-nosed friend with you."

Billy and Sammy took off at a run. They were almost home free when they ran smack into the air-raid warden.

"Stop in the name of the law!" he hollered. "You're under arrest for breaking curfew!"

"Aw, who says so?" sauced Billy, feeling invincible

after escaping the slammer. "You can't arrest us. You're not a policeman."

"And besides, this here's Swansea, not Toronto. So there!" yelled a suddenly brave Sammy.

Then they broke into a run again and didn't stop until they were in front of Sammy's house.

"I'll get killed when Mr. Thunder phones my dad," he said, his eyes welling up with tears again.

"Don't worry. He won't phone," Billy assured him. "The Thunders never snitch on anybody."

Billy was right about that. But he and Sammy were both punished, anyway, for staying out so late and worrying their mothers into their graves.

Chapter 17

Summer Holidays

Finally summer arrived. Jakey was invited to spend the holidays with cousins in Port Credit, so Billy took the opportunity to make extra money by doing Jakey's paper route as well as his own.

One hot July afternoon, when the heat bugs were singing in the trees and black tar was bubbling up between the cracks in the sidewalk, Billy came panting in the kitchen door after finishing both routes.

"There's a letter for you on the hall table, Bingo," his mother said, tears streaming down her face from the onions she was chopping on the cutting board.

"From Arthur?" Billy asked hopefully.

His sailor brother had not answered his long letter, so, true to his word, Billy had not written to him again.

"No. It's postmarked Muskoka, so it must be from your Aunt Aggie."

Billy dropped Jakey's route bag on a chair and handed his mother a leftover *Evening Telegram*.

Lifting the lid of the wooden icebox, Mrs. Thomson placed a bowl of potato salad on top of the fast-melting ice. Then she spread the newspaper out on the kitchen table and read the headlines out loud:

ROYAL CANADIAN NAVY PUTS ARMY
ASHORE ON FRENCH BEACHES.

"Oh, the dear Lord have mercy," she murmured. Then she closed her eyes, and Billy knew his mother was praying for Arthur. He felt a twinge of guilt about not having written again.

* * *

Billy retrieved his letter from the hall table and ripped it open. Sure enough, it was from Aunt Aggie. She was his dad's only living sister, now that Nellie and May were dead.

> *Heckley, Muskoka,*
> *July 18, 1944.*

Hello there, Laddie Buck!
I received a few lines from your dad, day before yesterday, and he says you stood first again. Good for you! You must've inherited

your brains from yours truly! Ha! Ha!

*Well, it's eleven o'clock at night and I'm just
sitting here by my lonesome in the lamplight
ruminating on my day's work. I filled a big
honey pail with huckleberries this a.m., and
they put me in mind of you. Remember when you
were a little tad and I used to call you Blueberry
Eyes? It suited you to a T, too.*

*It was hot as Hades in the berry patch
today, so I went over to Miller's pond to
cool off and pull some bulrushes. The pond
water is as warm as silt and the Raggett
boys were up to their old shenanigans
jumping off Sheer Rock Cliff into the black
hole. They haven't got the sense God gave
fishing worms, them two.*

Billy grimaced at the mention of the Raggett
boys. The last time he had been to Muskoka they had
waylaid him at the pond, called him a city slicker,
and beat him up.

*I was just sitting here wondering if you'd
like to come up and visit me for a spell. You
could bring a friend if you like. There's lots of
beds in the attic. And if you can't cadge a ride
with someone coming north, maybe your ma
would let you take the train and I'd have the
mail truck pick you up in Huntsville. It meets
the four o'clock every day, so it wouldn't be
putting anybody out.*

Well, Laddie Buck, this old spinster is looking forward to seeing you. The log house has been mighty lonely since we planted your grandpa. He was a cranky old codger, and that's a fact, but I miss him like an itch.

I finally found a stone that suits me to mark the grave: a perfectly smooth fieldstone that looks like a giant toadstool. I stumbled on it, literally (stubbed my big toe), while I was foraging in the bush for mint and sage and saffron leaves. Had good pickings and found a nice wad of spruce gum to boot.

The next day, Angus Belcher came up to help me saw and stack wood. So I persuaded him (didn't take much persuading — I think he's sweet on me, tee-hee!) to help me fetch the stone on his grass sled. Had a nice ride. Haven't had a grass-sled ride since I sold Major to a nice family in Burk's Falls that wanted a gentle animal for their wee lad.

I miss Major. I do. It don't seem natural — a farm without a horse. But when I stopped doing my own haying, I reckoned I couldn't afford to keep him just for the friendship.

Tell Bea he's found a good home. She'll be relieved. She was always worried he'd end up in the glue factory. Bea set such store by that old work horse. Thought he was a prize stallion, she did.

*I still got my bossy old cow, though. She's
mean as dirt, but she's a good milker. And I've
got fourteen laying hens, two roosters, and an
ornery old goose. And my vegetable patch is
plentiful this year, so you won't go hungry.*

*Well the oil's gone low in the lamp, so I'll
sign off now and take these weary bones to bed.
I'll look forward to hearing from you by return
mail.*

Lovingly,
Aunt Aggie.

Billy gave the letter to his mother.

"Not a word of greeting to anybody," she complained after she'd skimmed it. "She didn't even ask
after Arthur."

Handing it back, she returned to the paper. War
news always put her in a bad mood, especially if it
involved the navy.

"Can I go, Mum?"

"I don't know anybody going north right now," his
mother hedged.

"But Aunt Aggie says I could go by train. I'd like
that."

"I'm short of money," Mrs. Thomson hedged some
more.

"I can pay my own way. I got lots of money."

"What about your paper routes? And what about
your swimming lessons? Mr. Vierkoetter gave Bea a
ride home the other day, and he told her you're the

best in your class. He says if you keep it up, you've got a good chance to win a medal in the fall city competition."

"I'll find someone to do my paper routes for me, and I can practise swimming in Miller's Pond. Mr. Vierkoetter said we won't start training for the competition until August. Gee whiz!" He slumped on a chair and stuck out his bottom lip. "You treat me like a baby. I never have any fun. All I get to do is work."

He felt his mother's eyes upon him, so he continued to sulk at the floor.

Mrs. Thomson folded the paper and put it aside. Then she got cutlery out of the drawer and began setting the table.

"Yas, Bingo," she said thoughtfully, "you do need a holiday. You're skinny as a rake. Maybe all that food Aggie's bragging about will put some meat on your bones. Mind you, she's no great shakes as a cook. I remember once, when she was here, she offered to do my Saturday baking.

"She made two gooseberry pies and set them on the window sill to cool. Well, Booky and Arthur were fighting and chasing each other around the kitchen and they accidentally knocked one of the pies onto the floor. Upon my word, that pie was solid as a rock. Not so much as a crack in the crust. So don't expect the kind of meals you get here."

"I won't, Mum. Gee thanks, Mum. I've never been on a train by myself before."

"Well, since Aggie says you can bring a friend, I'll ask Mrs. Watson if Sammy can go with you. There's safety in numbers."

That gave Billy an idea.

"Maybe it would be even safer if I took Sammy *and* Hawk," he exclaimed.

"For land's sake, no. That would be too much of a good thing. You'll have to choose between them."

Oh, boy, thought Billy to himself, for once I get to choose. Usually Danny decides everything and Sammy and I have no say. It might serve Hawk right if I pick Sammy, except Hawk would be more fun.

It was going to be a tough decision.

* * *

That night the three boys went biking down on the lakeshore.

They stopped at the railway tracks and hopped off their bikes. Kneeling on their hands and knees in the cinders, they all pressed their ears on the steel ribbon, held their breath and listened.

After a few moments Billy stood up, brushed the cinders off his pants and said, "I don't hear anything."

"Me neither," agreed Sammy.

"Shut up!" Danny hissed and kept his ear on the rail.

After a few more moments he got up and said, "A train'll be here in ten minutes."

They waited while Sammy counted the minutes on his pocket watch, and sure enough, exactly ten minutes later a train went whistling by.

"How'd you know, Hawk?" Sammy asked.

"It's easy when you're a Mohawk," Danny said proudly.

Picking up their bikes, they pushed them across Lakeshore Road and sat on the soft warm sand of Sunnyside beach.

Lake Ontario glittered like a pan of gold in the sunset. Shading their eyes, they gazed out across the blue water, trying to see Buffalo on the American side.

All of a sudden, Sammy jumped up and let out a loud snort.

"Hey, look!" he cried, pointing towards the middle of the lake. "Ain't that a periscope out there?"

Running to the water's edge, they cupped their hands around their eyes and stared out past the breakwater.

Sure enough, near the horizon they saw a mysterious object bobbing up and down in the choppy waves.

"I'm pretty sure it's a German U-boat," Billy said.

"What makes you think so?" asked a sceptical Hawk.

" 'Cause my brother's in the navy."

Danny couldn't argue with that, so they kept on staring until the object disappeared as mysteriously as it had appeared.

"We better report it to the coast guard," Sammy said.

"You're nuts," Danny said. "It's probably just an old rowboat or a log or something."

"Yeah," Billy agreed. "Maybe it was just an optical illusion. Nobody else seemed to notice it."

There were a few bathers still cavorting in the water.

"I wish I'd brought my bathing suit," lamented Billy.

"If we wait until dark, we can go in in our underwears," suggested Sammy.

"I don't wear no underwears," Hawk said.

"No kidding!" snorted Sammy.

"Wanna make something out of it?" growled Hawk.

"Heck no. We can't stay out that late, anyway, on account of the curfew." Sammy picked up his bike and brushed sand off the saddle. "Besides, none of that matters to me. Our family's going to my uncle's cottage on Sturgeon Lake and the water's a lot warmer there."

The moment he heard this, a light popped on in Billy's head.

"When are you going?" he asked casually.

"Saturday," replied Sammy smugly. "We're staying for two whole weeks."

Billy could hardly keep the grin off his face. The minute they parted company with Sammy, he said to Danny, "My Aunt Aggie has invited me to Muskoka for my holidays, Hawk, and she says I can bring a friend. Wanna come?"

"Sure." Danny's black eyes glowed with excitement. "I've never been out of the city in my whole life before. What's there to do up there, Stretch?"

"Lots of stuff," Billy bragged. "You'll see."

Chapter 18

Muskoka

Billy and Danny arrived in Hunstville by train the day after Sammy left for Sturgeon Lake. Sure enough, a battered old mail truck with a faded royal emblem on the side was waiting for them at the station.

Billy leapt down the train's iron steps and hollered, "Hi, Bertha!"

Landing in a puff of dust beside him, Danny exclaimed, "Holy geez, a mail lady."

"Halloo there, stranger!" greeted Bertha, her grizzled grey hair sticking out in swatches from beneath her official cap. "How's the weather up there?" Shading her eyes she looked up at Billy. "My how you've growed," she exclaimed. "Tall and skinny as a beanpole."

She noticed Danny standing beside him.

"And how are you doing down there, Shorty?"

Danny stuck out his chest like an angry rooster. "The name's Thunder," he snapped.

Bertha guffawed and jumped into the cab of the truck, motioning Danny to hop in beside her.

"Sounds Indian to me," she said.

"It is . . . Mohawk."

Danny's black eyes flashed defiantly and he stared straight ahead out the windshield.

"Me too! My great-grandma. Put 'er there, pardner!" And they shook hands like long-lost cousins.

Squeezing in beside Danny, Billy crossed his long legs and managed to clank the door shut.

"I never knew you were part Indian, Bertha," he said, sounding disgruntled.

"There's lots of things you don't know, Sonny Boy," she chuckled as she let out the clutch and stepped on the gas.

For the next twenty miles, as they bumped over the rocky road to Heckley, Bertha and Danny swapped Indian stories. Pretty soon Billy was fed up because he couldn't get a word in edgewise. He was glad when they finally rounded the red dirt turning and the log house came into view.

There was Aunt Aggie, as tall and lean and tanned as Billy remembered her, whipping off her sugar bag apron and sticking a long hairpin into the straw-coloured bun on top of her head.

"Hi, Aunt Aggie!"

Billy's spirits rose at the homely sight of her. Jumping out of the mail truck before it had time to stop, he ran straight into her outstretched arms.

After a breathtaking hug, Billy introduced Aunt Aggie to Danny and the three of them waved goodbye to Bertha as she took off in a cloud of dust.

Picking up their grips from where Bertha had dropped them in the clover, Aggie led the way into the log house.

It was two years since Billy had been to Muskoka, and during that time the house seemed to have shrunk. The doorway was so low that both he and his aunt had to duck their heads to enter. Only Danny was able to step inside without stooping.

The daylight filtering through the wavery windowpanes lit the room dimly. It took a few minutes for their eyes to adjust to the subdued light.

Finally Billy was able to gaze around at the rough pine walls, the old-fashioned pictures, the homemade wooden furniture.

"Geez, it hasn't changed a bit," he said nostalgically.

Danny whistled softly. "I feel like I just went backwards about a hundred years," he said softly.

Aggie chuckled at this remark. "That's about as old as everything is in this big old house," she said.

"Now you two go out back and wash up and I'll get supper on the table."

Billy led the way through the woodshed and out the back door. A rainbarrel stood under the eavestrough, a long-handled dipper hooked over the rim. Beside it on a sun-bleached bench was a chipped enamel basin and a cake of yellow soap.

Billy dipped amber coloured water from the rainbarrel into the basin.

Danny stared into the shallow water. "What's those wiggly things in there?" he asked suspiciously.

Billy laughed. "They're mosquitoes that haven't hatched yet. Don't worry, they won't bite."

The yellow soap frothed up in the soft rainwater. They washed, then dried on a flannel cloth that hung from a wooden peg sticking out of the log house.

* * *

For supper they had chicken roasted in the woodstove, baby potatoes boiled in their jackets, new carrots, and fiddlehead ferns that looked like curled up green worms. Both boys pushed aside the fiddleheads.

"Eat your greens!" ordered Aggie. "I foraged for miles in the bush to find them for you. They're scarce as hen's teeth this late in the season."

So they washed down the greens with great gulps of foamy milk and mopped their plates with thick chunks of homemade bread.

"What's for dessert, Aunt Aggie?" asked Billy.

Aggie grinned and the crow's feet around her sparkly eyes crinkled like crepe paper. "How does thimbleberries and cream tickle your fancy?"

"Swell!" answered Danny before Billy had a chance to say anything.

"Well, then, Laddie Buck" — Billy glanced up sharply and saw that his aunt was talking to Danny, even though she had used *his* nickname — "Bingo can take you down to the spring to fetch the cream. I'll clear the table and dish up the berries."

The spring was at the bottom of the hillpath behind the house. Crystal clear water poured out of a copper pipe into a wooden tub. Wavery outlines of bottles could be seen in through the gurgling water. Danny plunged in his arm and came up with a pint of yellow cream.

"Holy cow, that water's cold!" he cried.

"It's always like that," said Billy, "no matter how hot the weather gets. And in winter it never ices over."

"How come?"

"Because it comes from so deep in the ground," Billy explained, proud of his country knowledge.

Aggie whipped the cream with a fork and heaped it on the wine-coloured berries. Both boys had two heaping helpings.

"Mmmm! That stuff's better than ice cream," declared Danny, licking the white moustache off his upper lip.

"That's because Bossy just made it for you this a.m.," grinned Aggie.

"Who's Bossy?" asked Danny curiously.

"She's my old cow," explained Aggie. "I didn't give her a proper name because I don't like her much. Too bossy. Want to come with me to the barn while I milk her?"

"Sure," cried Danny eagerly.

On the way down the weedy path to the barn, Aggie said to Danny, "Billy said you're part Mohawk. There's Mohawks around these parts. They live by tracking and trapping. You do any tracking?"

"Nope. There's no place to track in the city."

"Except the railway tracks," put in Billy. "Hawk can lean his ear on the track and tell exactly when the train's coming, even if it's twenty miles away."

"Then you got the gift," said Aggie.

She unlatched the barn's half-door and they followed her to the stall. Bossy's moo changed to an indignant bellow when Aggie pushed her aside, sat on a stool, pressed her forehead against the cow's brown flank and began squirting milk with a singing rhythm into a metal pail.

Danny watched fascinated. He had never seen milk outside of a Silverwood's bottle before.

When the pail was full, the two boys followed Aggie to the henhouse. "Might as well gather our breakfast," she said.

The hens were all nesting, their eyelids half shut.

"Hello there, girls," whispered Aggie soothingly.

The hens blinked and chittered softly as she slipped her hand under their feathers.

"And how's my Hester?" she asked a puffy red hen. Hester wiggled down and got more comfortable on her eggs. Aggie didn't slip her hand under Hester.

"She's broody," she explained. (Sure enough, a few days later, three yellow chicks appeared.)

The boys cradled the warm brown eggs in their cupped hands and Aggie carried the milk pail.

"I never seen brown eggs before," Danny remarked.

"They're better for you than white," Aggie said, "They're chock full of vit-a-mins."

"I only saw one rooster, Aunt Aggie," remarked Billy. "In your letter you said you had two."

Aggie gave a little snicker as they followed her back up the path to the loghouse.

"You et the other one for supper," she said.

Chapter 19

Ghost Stories

That night, when darkness crept into the old loghouse, Aggie lit the big oil lamp and turned the wick up as high as it would go without smoking.

"You two set here while I slide down to the spring for the sarsaparilla," Aggie said.

"What's sarsaparilla?" asked Danny.

"You'll see," she grinned, lighting the lantern. Then she ducked her head and disappeared out the door.

When she returned, they all sat cosily around the oilcloth covered table in the circle of light.

Aunt Susan had sent up a generous bag of her best nut mixture with Billy — an annual gift to Aunt Aggie — so they nibbled on giant cashews, Brazil nuts and pecans while they sipped tangy, ice-cold sarsaparilla.

"Well, how do you like my homemade soda pop?" Aggie asked.

"It's terrific!" Danny took another long swig. "What's it made of?"

"Roots from the sarsaparilla shrub," explained Aggie, crunching a Brazil nut. "I boil them down to a syrup with honey and fresh spring water."

Danny looked at Billy with raised eyebrows.

"If we took some of them roots home, I bet my old man could make a fortune," he said.

"Is your father a confectioner like Billy's Aunt Susan?" asked Aggie.

"Heck no," Billy butted in. "Mr. Thunder's a bootlegger."

He glanced at Danny and saw that if looks could kill, he'd be dead as a doornail.

"Sounds like an interesting occupation," Aggie said without so much as batting an eyelash.

The night air coming in the window had turned cool, so Aggie made a small fire in the woodstove. The dry timber sparked and crackled and the lamp flared and flickered, casting long shadows on the walls.

"Tell us a story, Aunt Aggie," begged Billy, remembering what a swell storyteller she was. "Tell us about the time great-aunt Polly's ghost came to visit."

"Well, it was more of a vision than a visitation," Aggie began, her voice lowering to a whisper. "One night, my grandma, that's her up there," she pointed to the portrait of a wrinkled old lady in an oval frame, "woke up out of a sound sleep and sat bolt upright in bed. There in the doorway stood her sister Polly, who she hadn't set eyes on for nigh on twenty years.

"Now she knew her sister was far across the sea in England, yet there she stood, large as life in the old log house."

Danny shivered and whispered, "Was she a ghost?"

"Not according to Grandma. She was as real as you and me. Though she had no proof, because Grandpa slept right through it. Anyway, Polly spoke to her, and this is what she said."

Aggie's voice changed to a soft trill. "'Tis I, meself, Sophie. I've come to bid thee farewell.' Then she pointed with a transparent finger — that's what Grandma said — to Grandpa's pocket watch ticking on the washstand. So Grandma picked it up and saw in the eerie light that it was exactly two o'clock in the morning. Then Polly whispered faintly, for she was fading fast, 'Goodbye, Sophie. God bless. 'Til we meet again.' And with that, pouf, she was gone."

"Tell the rest, Aunt Aggie! Tell the rest!" begged Billy, "It's my favourite part."

Aggie nibbled another nut and took a sip of sarsaparilla, then she continued.

"Well, no one believed poor old grandma. They said she was having delusions. Until six weeks later, when a letter edged in black arrived from Polly's husband, Peter. He wrote that Polly had departed this life, and it turned out that the moment of her departure was exactly the same moment that Grandma had had her vision."

"Wow!" breathed Danny. "Tell us another one, Aunt Aggie."

Billy felt a sharp stab of jealousy. Did Hawk *have* to call her Aunt Aggie, even if she did not object? She was Billy's aunt, not Danny's.

Aggie added a few dry sticks to the red ashes in the stove. They snapped and crackled and orange flames shot up, casting a storytelling glow over the kitchen.

"I remember like it was yesterday," she said, sitting back down in the circle of light, "the night the organ in the parlour — brought all the way from Nottingham in 1872 — began playing Brahms' 'Lullaby'. And at the very same moment, the grandfather clock, that one right there in the corner, struck three. We didn't know what woke us, the clock or the music, so we all crept down the stairs after Papa to see who was playing our organ.

"But as soon as Papa opened the parlour door, the music stopped. And we could see by the moonlight coming in the window that the closed lid that covered the ivory keys was still woven shut with cobwebs."

Billy and Danny shivered and begged for more. So Aggie told another story, and then another. In no time at all, the grandfather clock was striking eleven and Aggie declared it was time for bed.

With a big sigh, Aggie pushed herself up from the table and lit the lantern again so the boys could find their way to the outhouse.

Halfway down the dewy path they stopped to gaze up at the star-spangled, black-velvet sky.

"Geez!" Danny marvelled, "I never seen so many stars. There must be billions."

"Trillions," corrected Billy.

"Whew!" whistled Danny.

Inside the outhouse, Billy set the lantern between the two round holes.

"You gotta watch how you sit, Hawk," he said.

"I don't need to sit," Danny said.

"Well, when you do, be careful."

"Why?"

" 'Cause you might get splinters."

"How come?"

"Raccoons. This here's where they sharpen their teeth."

Just then they heard the sharp snap of a twig breaking. Looking fearfully over their shoulders, they stared out into the moon-washed bush lot.

"What's that?" hissed Danny.

"Maybe a bear," Billy said.

Bumping into each other, they made a mad dash for the house.

Bursting through the woodshed door, Billy cried, "We think we heard a bear, Aunt Aggie!"

"Did you see him?" she asked.

"No. But we heard him plain as day."

"Sounds like Big Foot. Where's the lantern?"

"We forgot it."

The two boys watched anxiously from the doorway as Aggie went chortling down the path.

When she came back with the lantern she said, "Well, you must have scared him off, because I only saw a big old skunk. Lucky for me we're friends, else I'd be stinking to high heaven right now."

Now she lit a candle stuck in a mound of melted wax on a saucer and handed it to Billy.

"Goodnight. Sweet repose. Sleep on your back so you won't squash your nose," she chanted.

Laughing, they made their way up the dark stairwell to one of the attic bedrooms. Aunt Aggie had put them in the same room so they wouldn't be lonely.

Billy set the saucer on the washstand and they got into their pyjamas in the flickering light. They climbed into bed and the mattress crunched and crackled under them.

"What the heck's in there?"

"Straw." Billy leaned over and blew out the candle. "If you think this is bad, you ought to try the one in the next room. It's stuffed with dried cornhusks."

The two boys lay on their backs, their hands clasped behind their heads, staring up at the sloping rafters. Moonbeams sprayed the room with pale light and lit up the only picture on the wall: a portrait in an oval frame of a girl with a high lace collar, swept-up hair and large round eyes that gazed intently down upon them.

"Hey!" Danny whispered. "She looks like your sister Bea. And she's staring right at us."

"That's my Aunt Nellie," Billy explained. "She died before I was born. Her eyes follow you wherever you go. The picture used to hang in the parlour, but Aunt Aggie found herself starting to talk to her, so she moved it up here, out of sight. They were awful close when they were girls, Aunt Aggie said."

They fell silent then, listening to the night noises that floated through the mosquito netting covering the window: whispering pines, lowing cows, hooting owls, a lone wolf baying at the moon. Then another sharp crack.

They turned and stared at each other, their eyes glistening in the moonlight. Big Foot?

Danny scrunched down under the summer quilt and the mattress snapped and crackled.

"Geez, Stretch," he said excitedly, "I ain't never going to sleep tonight."

Two minutes later, both he and Billy were snoring contentedly.

Chapter 20

Kinfolk

Cock-a-doodle-do!

The surviving rooster woke the boys at the crack of dawn. Leaping out of bed, they jumped into their clothes and hurried down the stairs.

"Good morning, my Buckos!" Aggie was standing on a chair tacking a new flypaper to the beam above the table. No sooner had the sticky yellow ribbon unfurled than three flies landed on it feet first, their wings whirring madly.

Climbing down, she asked Danny, "And how did you sleep your first night in the country, Laddie Buck?"

"Like a log," Danny answered, flexing his muscles.

Aggie nodded her approval, then began filling

their plates with fluffy eggs and crackly bacon from an iron frying pan.

When breakfast was done, Aggie put on her straw hat and got a spade from the woodshed.

"I've got to dig potatoes this a.m.," she said. "Got to get them into the root cellar before the frost. Frost comes early in this neck of the woods."

"Can we help, Aunt Aggie?" offered Billy.

"No, thanks just as much. Why, don't you take your friend down the road to visit your kinfolk?"

* * *

The road was a narrow wagon trail that wound through a tunnel of trees. It was alive with a million little creatures and insects.

"I thought you said your aunt lived up here all alone, Stretch." Danny brushed flying grasshoppers out of his hair. "I don't want to meet a bunch of strangers."

"Don't worry, Hawk, you'll like them." Billy caught a shiny black cricket and gave it a ride on his shoulder.

Danny stopped and looked up through a sudden break in the trees. A flaky white cloud was drifting through a patch of brilliant blue sky.

"It sure is swell up here, Stretch," he said, taking a deep breath of pure country air. "I feel like I belong here already."

* * *

At a sharp bend in the road, the steeple of an old stone church rose out of the dense green forest. Beside it, overgrown with weeds, was a dilapidated pioneer cemetery.

The rusty iron gate creaked as Billy pulled it open.

"Why are we going in here?" Danny took a step backward. "I hate graveyards. They give me the creeps."

Billy laughed a witchy laugh.

" 'Cause this is where my kinfolk live," he whispered in a cackly voice.

"Cut that out, Stretch," Danny snapped.

Most of the graves were sunken and hidden by weeds. One mushroom-shaped stone with neatly trimmed grass and flowers growing around it stood out. Carefully printed in white paint on the stone were the names of Billy's ancestors.

Pointing to each name, Billy explained who they used to be. But Danny wasn't paying attention. He kept glancing nervously over his shoulder.

"Let's get outta here," he said.

They spent the rest of the morning exploring the countryside.

* * *

In the afternoon, after a hearty noontime meal, Aggie ducked her head through the woodshed door and came back carrying a rifle and a hatchet.

"Okey-doke, my Buckos," she said. "Follow me!"

"Where to?" asked Danny.

"You'll see," she said with a mischievous grin.

Off they went with Aggie in the lead, her long strides cutting a path through the wilderness.

They trekked for miles through bush so dense and dark that only occasionally a shaft of sunlight managed to penetrate through the trees. Several times Aunt Aggie had to hack their way through vines as thick as ropes.

Then suddenly, as if by magic, they stepped out of the forest into a clearing. Before them spread a grassy field, undulating with a hundred windswept mounds.

"What are all those little hills?" asked Danny in a whisper.

"They're Mohawk graves. This is an Indian burial ground." Aggie took off her straw hat and held it over her heart respectfully. "I reckoned since you'd paid a visit to Billy's kin, that you might like to pay some homage to your own folk."

Danny stood still as a statue. Billy glanced sideways at his profile. Gosh, he thought, if Hawk had on a feathered headdress, he'd look just like that picture of Chief Thundercloud on the Thunders' wall.

At that moment, the sound of something big crashing through the trees came to them from the other side of the field.

They looked up and there, staring straight across the golden graveyard, stood a huge black bear on hind legs, growling ominously.

"It's him," breathed Danny. "It's Big Foot!"

"Don't move a muscle," whispered Aggie.

Danny grabbed Billy's arm and Billy covered his hand in a tight grip. Out of the corner of his eye he saw his aunt slowly easing the barrel of the rifle up from where it was pointing to the ground.

Minutes dragged by like hours. The skeeters (Aunt Aggie's word for mosquitos) had a picnic, and they didn't dare to swat.

The bear was being tormented too. Weaving his head from side to side, he swiped with his paws at the cloud of bloodthirsty insects swarming about his ears.

Suddenly he let out an anguished roar that made the three explorers jump in spite of themselves. Then he dropped to all fours, wheeled around and went crashing back into the forest.

"Whew!" breathed Aggie, lowering the gun.

Billy looked admiringly at his intrepid aunt. "Would the rifle have killed him, Aunt Aggie?" he asked.

"No better than a slingshot," she said. "But it

might've scared him some. C'mon, let's make tracks for home."

Safely back in the old log house, Danny said, "Thanks for taking me to that place, Aunt Aggie. It was kind of spooky, but I'm glad I saw it, and I'm sure glad we got to see Big Foot. I wasn't even scared."

Bull, thought Billy to himself.

Chapter 21

Getting Even

Billy and Danny had been in Muskoka for over a week and had done just about everything. Today was the hottest day of the year and they sat in the shade of the house on a half-log bench, groaning and rubbing their stomachs after one of Aunt Aggie's homegrown noonday dinners.

Her cooking might not compare to Mum's, Billy thought, but it sure comes in a close second.

"What'll we do this aft?" asked Danny, rolling a spitball around in his mouth.

Beads of sweat ran down Billy's face to his shirt collar, where they were soaked up like a blotter.

"Let's go swimming in Miller's Pond. That'll cool us off. And I promised my mum I'd keep in practice."

"I hate swimming," objected Danny. "And besides, we ain't got bathing suits."

"Up here you can swim in your skin," laughed Billy.

"Ya, well I ain't in the mood."

"You're never in the mood," complained Billy. "Every time I suggest something, you say no."

Danny blew the spitball out of his mouth and it hit the fence with a splat.

"Okay, okay, I'll go. But I ain't getting wet."

"Swell!" Billy jumped up. "I'll go tell Aunt Aggie."

His aunt was churning butter in her grandmother's old wooden churn.

"Well, I guess it's all right," she agreed reluctantly, "but don't jump into the black hole. Just swim in the pond."

Aggie lifted the lid of the churn to check the butter's progress. Creamy yellow curds clung to the paddle and thin white whey streamed back into the churn. She nodded her head in satisfaction.

"I'll have some nice fresh buttermilk cooling in the spring when you get back," she promised. Then she added, "And mind you give those Raggett boys a wide berth. They're mean as weasels when it comes to city slickers."

"Aw, don't worry about them, Miss Thomson," Danny said, and he stuck out his arms, clenched his fists and bulged his biceps. "I can take care of them."

"I'll just bet you can," Aggie laughed, reaching

over to feel his arm muscles. "Like a brick," she said. "And there you go calling me Miss again. How many times do I have to tell you to call me Aunt like Billy does?"

"Sorry, Aunt Aggie." Danny flashed a rare smile. "I ain't never had a aunt before."

"Well, let's go if we're going," scowled Billy.

*   *   *

Miller's Pond was as smooth as glass. Billy leaned down and swished his hand back and forth, rippling the green water.

"It's as warm as silt," he said. He shaded his eyes and looked up to the top of Sheer Rock cliff. No one was there. "Let's go up," he suggested.

Danny followed his gaze. "What for?" he said.

"To look around. You can see for miles up there. C'mon, Hawk. You're not afraid, are you?"

"I ain't afraid of nothing," Danny retorted. "And don't you forget it."

A path wound its way up one side of the cliff. Danny followed Billy reluctantly up the steep, winding path, grabbing onto hardy little spruce trees that grew in the cracks.

At last they reached the summit and pulled themselves onto the flat top of the cliff. They sat for a moment to catch their breath. Then Billy jumped to his feet and walked fearlessly over to the cliff's edge.

"Come and look, Hawk," he said. "You can tell the

earth is round from way up here. It's amazing."

But Danny stayed put, sitting on a boulder that was hot enough to fry eggs on.

Sensing Danny's fear, Billy began to show off. Rising up on his toes, he spread out his arms like an eagle.

"C'mon, Hawk," he urged. "You gotta see this. There's a rainbow arcing right across the horizon."

Hesitantly Danny made his way over to the brink. But instead of looking out at the vast blue sky, he looked down to the still black pool below.

"Isn't it fantastic?" Billy enthused, glancing at Danny to see his reaction. Danny's brown face had turned strangely pale and he stood as still as a statue.

"What's the matter, Hawk?" Billy asked, and when Danny didn't answer, he said, "Wanna see me jump?"

"Why would anybody be dumb enough to jump?"

"Because it's fun. It feels like flying. You aren't scared, are you, Hawk?"

"I ain't scared of nothing!" snapped Danny angrily.

"Then let's see ya jump, wiseguy!"

The voice seemed to have come out of nowhere. Then a redheaded boy hoisted himself onto the top of the cliff, followed by two others.

It was the Raggetts. Turning to face them, all the bravado went out of Billy. But Danny automatically raised his fists, ready for action. This was the kind of challenge that was right up his alley.

Suddenly Billy was doubly glad that he had invited Danny to Muskoka, and not Sammy.

One thing he was sure of, it would take more than three Raggetts brothers to get the best of one Hawk Thunder.

Red Raggett, the biggest of the three, took a step forward, closing the gap between them.

All of a sudden, without warning, Red lowered his head like a mountain goat and butted Danny right in the stomach.

Taken completely by surprise, Danny lost his balance and plunged backwards over the precipice.

"YIIIII!"

His terrified scream trailed after him as he plummeted downward.

Before Billy's horrified eyes, Danny hit the water and disappeared.

Holding his breath, he watched and waited for his friend to surface. At last Danny's head bobbed up and he began thrashing crazily in the dark water.

"HELP, STRETCH! HELP! I CAN'T SWIM!"

Hawk's terrified cries echoed off the rocks, then down he went for the second time.

Without hesitation, Billy leapt off the cliff, feet first.

The hole was incredibly deep. Billy sank like a

stone into its dark depths. Then he fought his way to the surface and trod water, looking for Danny. But he was nowhere in sight. Billy filled his lungs with air and dove straight down again.

Opening his eyes wide, he could just make out Danny's black hair waving amongst the water weeds. Reaching out he grabbed a handful and pushed with all his might for the surface.

At last his head broke free. A split second later, Danny's head burst out of the water beside him.

Gulping for air, Danny began thrashing like a wild thing.

"Stop, Hawk! Stop!" cried Billy.

But in his frenzy Danny continued to struggle, dragging them both underwater.

Again Billy fought his way upwards, and this time Danny wasn't struggling. He had gone as limp as a rag doll.

It took every ounce of Billy's strength and willpower to drag Danny's body — a dead weight — up onto the grassy bank. Exhausted, he flopped down beside Danny, gasping for air, his heart pounding like a sledgehammer. Then, as his breathing slowed, he glanced over at his friend.

Danny lay perfectly still, his eyes closed.

"Hawk!" Billy felt a stab of fear. "HAWK!" he cried again. But Danny didn't stir.

Kneeling over his friend, Billy shook him by the shoulders. Danny's head flopped lifelessly from side to side. Frantically Billy began slapping his friend's pale cheeks.

"Aw, c'mon, Hawk!" he begged, a sob welling up in his throat. But Danny remained motionless.

Suddenly Billy knew what he had to do. With a new surge of energy he rolled Danny over and straddled his back. Turning Danny's face to one side he folded his friend's arms above his head. Then he spread his own hands on Danny's back and began pumping. He had not had lifesaving lessons yet, but he had watched Mr. Vierkoetter teaching it.

"C'mon, Hawk, breathe," he begged as he kept up the rhythmic motion.

Water began gushing from Danny's mouth with every push.

"Please, Hawk." He was counting now. "Ten, eleven, twelve . . . thirty, thirty-one . . . "

Was that a moan he heard? Billy redoubled his efforts. All of a sudden Danny let out a loud, watery belch.

As he rolled his friend over on his back, Billy saw two big black eyes staring up at him, still filled with terror.

"Are you okay now, Hawk?" He swallowed a sob.

Slowly, Danny raised himself up on shaky elbows.

"Yeah, I'm okay," he said, and Billy heaved a sigh of relief.

Then Danny's shining black eyes looked deep into

his friend's worried blue ones and he said in a surprised voice, "You know something, Stretch? You saved my life. And to a Mohawk that means you own me."

Billy stared back at him with a puzzled frown and gave an embarrassed laugh.

"To me it just means we're even," he said.

Bernice Thurman Hunter developed an interest in writing in early childhood, and when her own children were small, she wrote stories for them. But it was not until her children were grown up that she began to have her work published. Many of Bernice's novels are autobiographical in nature, and one of her strengths as a writer is her ability to bring childhood memories vividly to life for her readers. Her books are enormously popular with readers of all ages.

Bernice has been the recipient of numerous awards, including the Vicky Metcalf Award (1990) and the 1981 IODE Award for *That Scatterbrain Booky*.